THE LIGHT IN THE SHADOWS
EL PACE

Copyright © 2025 by EL Pace

All rights reserved.

No portion of this book may be reproduced in any form without written permission from the publisher or author, except as permitted by U.S. copyright law.

CONTENTS

Dedication	1
Preface	2
Introduction	3
1. Skia	4
2. Seer	11
3. King Morthal	16
4. Skia	23
5. King Morthal	28
6. Meir	33
7. King Morthal	40
8. Skia	47
9. Skia	59
10. Skia	66

11.	Skia	72
12.	Meir	79
13.	Skia	84
14.	Skia	92
15.	Seer	97
16.	Meir	101
17.	Seer	106
18.	Meir	110
19.	Skia	115
20.	Skia	119
21.	Meir	124
22.	Skia	127
23.	Skia	134
24.	Meir	140
25.	Skia	146
26.	Skia	151
27.	Skia	155

28.	Skia	159
29.	Skia	163
30.	Meir	169
31.	Skia	179
32.	Meir	183
33.	Skia	187
34.	Skia	192
35.	Skia	197
36.	Skia	204
37.	Skia	212
38.	Seer	221
39.	Skia	225
40.	Meir	233
41.	Skia	237
42.	Skia	246
43.	Meir	251
44.	Meir	255

45. Meir	262
46. Meir	272
47. Skia	281
48. Meir	287
49. Skia	296
50. Seer	303
51. Skia	307
52. Skia	316
53. Meir	325
54. Meir	330
55. Lucile	335
56. Meir	340
57. Skia	342
58. Skia	345
Thank you.	353

To my husband, who, through all my shadows, found my light.

This is a story that walks in darkness, where cruelty and hope clash as characters fight for survival and change.

Please be aware that The Light in the Shadows contains dark themes including kidnapping, blood and gore, anxiety, fear, panic, dread, bullying, physical abuse, torture, violence, manipulation and death. While these elements are central to the journey, I understand they may be difficult for some readers.

Take care of yourself as you read and know it's okay to pause or step away if you need to.

With gratitude,

E.L. Pace

Dear Reader,

Thank you for stepping into the world of The Light in the Shadows. This story has lived in my heart for years, and I'm beyond grateful to share it with you. Within these pages, you'll meet Skia, a daughter of darkness standing at the edge of change, and walk with her through betrayal, magic and the fragile balance between light and shadow.

This book is the first step in the Born of Shadows series, and I couldn't be more excited that you're here at the very beginning of the journey. Whether you found this story through fantasy, tropes you love, or sheer curiosity, your presence means the world.

May you find light even in the darkest of places.

With love and gratitude,

E.L. Pace

ONE
SKIA

One wrong step and I'll join the bones scattered across the dungeon floor. They crunch beneath my imagination before I even touch them. My heart won't slow down.

It hammers and hammers as I creep down the side stairwell, every breath scraping in my throat. Each footfall echoes eerily in the silence, a rhythmic pulse against the pounding in my ears. The stone is slick and cold under my boots, and the air is heavy, as if it doesn't want me here. It remembers me. Each step brings me to a place I know I don't belong.

The deeper I descend, the more the walls close in. My skin prickles. Each step feels like trespass, like I'm entering the heart of something that was never meant to be uncovered.

The door waits in the shadows, tucked away like it knows it shouldn't exist. But I know it does, and I know it's calling me. Whispers of the shadows call to me. My fingers shake on the iron handle, the chill biting into my skin. It feels like grabbing a blade. I almost turn back. Almost. But the shadows in my blood laugh, daring me to open it.

You know the truth, Skia. Silly little girl.

I swat away the shadows as I push the door open. Hinges moan, and the smell hits me first, rot, wet earth, old bones. It's thick, like it wants to crawl down my throat and stay there. Rats skitter past my ankles, dragging scraps I don't dare identify. I breathe shallow, sharp breaths so I don't choke on it.

I descend one step at a time, trying not to make a sound, but the torch in my hand betrays me. Each step reminds me of my childhood. My hand grips the torch. The flame wobbles in the draft, threatening to die, and my shadows whisper in my ear, urging me to snuff it out, urging me to let them rise instead. They whisper what they'll do if I free them, promises too dark, too tempting, and I clench my jaw so hard it hurts. I won't. Not yet. Not here. Not again.

The stairwell splits, offering two distinct routes. Left. Right. The putrid reek of mold fills the air, causing my stomach to churn. I gag, stumble, and force myself upright. Left it is. The image of what could remain haunted me with each echo of my steps. The floor is a dark, glistening expanse. Water, I think, until the cold, clammy liquid seeps into my boots, a revolting stickiness. I don't want to know the source, or the smell.

The hall widens into an opening. I lift the torch higher, and light glints off chains surrounded by shadow where bones lie in ruin. Runes pulse in the stone, half-hidden under moss, as if alive. *Yes. We told you.* My hand trembles as I brush one clean. The slime clings, cloying, refusing to release my skin. A feeling of warmth washes over me, my palm's mark buzzes with a hidden anticipation, and I find myself smiling. An answer giving way past the grim on the walls.

Here are the runes that were in the book. The answer was here all along...

And then I hear it.

A scrape. A breath.

When I turn, I see them, eyes glowing orange-red, waiting in the dark.

My body stiffens. I press against the wall, cold moss soaking my back. My torchlight trembles across the shape of the thing, and the stench of it slams into me — death, old, and wet, worse than flesh left to rot. Its skin glistens, black muck dripping onto the stones. My stomach heaves. That wasn't water.

It opens its mouth. Teeth that are jagged, razored, and too many. It's huge, like a bear stripped of fur and mercy, every bone shoving against skin that sags and gleams. Shadows crawl over it. Stroke it. Feed it.

It roars.

The sound rips me in half. My ears ring, my knees slam into the stone as I clutch my head, my torch falling from my hands. I crawl blind, nails splitting against the wall, lungs burning. The shadows laugh in my head, shrieking louder than the creature. *Let us out and we'll end it. Let us out and we'll feast.*

Crawling. Stairs. My nails bite into the surface, and I haul myself up with a furious energy, my chest burning with a rage that fuels each aggressive climb. My knees bruise with each climb. I grabbed the stone wall, stumbling up.

Don't stop. Don't stop.

I slam into the door at the top, clawing for the handle. My fingers close around iron, freezing, and I wrench it open and slam it shut behind me. My body collapses against it, feeling fragile, unable to keep it shut. I command my shadows, and with a final thought, it closes.

Silence claps shut on the other side. The scream dies. Only my heart, beating like a drum, remains.

Each ragged breath is a struggle. My whole-body trembles. My father's secrets, his castle and his lies, twist around me like the shadows themselves. The runes were there the entire time. Creatures in the dungeon. Questions about my mother. And the shadows within me, whispering louder now, feed on my doubt.

I tiptoe through the halls like a child sneaking to bed past curfew, sweat sliding down my neck. Every corner is a threat. Every shadow, a whisper. My room, finally. I lock the door. The rushing of their voices quieted here.

This room was the only place in this castle where I never felt the castle's chill of fear.

The washroom steam fills my lungs, lavender and vanilla trying to drive out the dungeon's stench. Tears blur my eyes as I slide into the bath, water too hot, skin stinging, and chest aching.

The water is scalding. I want it to burn. To scald the dungeon off my skin, scorch the memory out of me. *The eyes, the runes, the chains, the scream.*

I slide under all the way, submerging the crown of my head, and wait for silence.

My shadows curl into my thoughts. Not soft at all.

We warned you, they murmur, smug as cats. *We would have kept you safe. We always will.*

"Liar," I mouth into the water. It floods my ears. The world goes far away.

He keeps secrets from you, they croon now, sweet, coaxing. *Let us have them. Let us devour the lies. Let us make you strong.*

Their voices tighten around me, seeping into the warmth until I can't tell what's water and what's shadow. Images flash through the dark. My father's silver eyes, Ashmore's gentle smile, Raven's fanged grin as she balanced on the library rail and dared me to jump. *You wouldn't,* she laughed. And then she jumped, and I followed, bruised both knees and lied about it. Raven's advice would be to open the door again. She would say, to run faster. She would demand the shadows to kneel. The creature would bend to her will.

My lungs ache. I break the surface with a gasp, water spilling down my face. The lamps blur, then steady. I'm shaking, and I hate it. I hate that the shadows feel it and like it.

The dungeon's silence, a vast, echoing emptiness, was more intense than the monster's menacing growl. My arms tremble as I sink lower into the tub, the blistering water cradling me like stone. My eyelids drag shut, too heavy to fight.

We're not done with you, they whisper, just as sleep pulls me under.

TWO
SEER

100 years ago

The wind howls like a living thing, a keening lament that tears through the stone spires of the ritual grounds. It whips my hair across my face and carries the acrid tang of smoke from the pyre that waits for me. Tonight, everything I am surrenders to the flame.

The fire roars in the center of the circle, an orange body with blue tongues lashing skyward, greedy for more. Shadows press close at the edges of the light; their twisting forms are hungry to watch a soul burn. Around me, the council of Seers stands cloaked in black, their hoods deep, their gazes unreadable. They all passed through this ritual once, and none of them bears the name they were born with. Each died and was reborn into silence, into service, into the eternal burden of sight.

My hands shake as I hold the parchment. My name brands the last trace of my old self. The quill scrapes across it moments before trembling as if it already knows it is etching its own grave. This is the last time my hand will form these letters. A name is more than a word, it is the memory of every person who ever speaks it, the echo of every laugh, every sorrow. Every love that I had before the path was chosen is given up. His silver eyes find me in the flame, and now I watch mine turn to ash.

The fire hisses as I cast it in. My name curls and blackens, shrinking upon itself, until nothing remains but sparks that rise into the dark sky. The sound it makes as it is consumed is almost a scream, so faint and fleeting I wonder if I only imagine it.

The High Seer steps forward. She is ancient, her back bent like a bow, her hair white and long, tangling in the wind. Her golden eyes glow unnaturally, twin lanterns in the night.

Around her thin throat hangs an amulet on a silver chain, and the emerald at its center pulses as though it has a heartbeat of its own. She removes it and presses it into my hands, and it is warm, as if fresh from flesh. My chest seizes, and my breath is stolen. The gem gleams brightly. So bright, I almost think I see the reflection of a child's eyes staring back at me. They are emerald eyes, sharp and alive, filled with a power that hasn't yet been born.

"Take it," the High Seer whispers, her voice sharp as broken glass. "This is the weight of centuries. Each life of ours pours into the stone. When one ends, another begins. From now until your bones return to the dust, you are bound."

I clasp the amulet around my neck. The metal bites into my skin.

She crumbles.

The High Seer's body dissolves into nothing, her flesh withering into a torrent of dust and light. Her soul surges into me, burning through my veins with a thousand futures. I stagger as visions strike like lightning, blistering behind my eyes.

A battlefield drowning in shadows.
A golden crown cast aside.
A girl with emerald eyes screaming in chains.
A prince ablaze in radiant light, his power scorching the

dark.

A betrayal. A knife. Blood.

I gasp, clawing at the air as my body convulses with the sheer force of it. Her voice—no, their voices—fill my head. Every Seer before me whispers in a chorus of prophecy. Too many. Too much.

The fire dies. Silence rushes in, oppressive and final. I stand alone in the circle, no longer myself, but something remade. My name is gone. My choices are gone. I am sight. I am burden. I am nothing but the vessel that carries the emerald's weight.

The other Seers bow their heads. None congratulate me. None embrace me. This is not a triumph. It is a sacrifice. They disappear into dust, their souls still hum around my neck.

I turn, my body heavy with the weight of all I now carry and walk from the circle. Their ghosts disappear into the dust that scatters the fire.

The forest opens its arms to me, its boughs bending low, whispering of the years to come. Waiting at the edge is a small stone cottage—mine now. My sanctuary. My prison. I reach for the iron latch, my hand trembling, and for the first time I feel truly hollow.

The emerald at my throat pulses once, twice, before settling into rhythm with my heartbeat. And in its glow, I glimpse again those eyes—the eyes of a child I do not know, but one whose fate will one day eclipse my own.

The wind howls again, carrying the sound of the Dark Forest's creatures, but in it I swear I hear a whisper.

She is coming.

THREE
KING MORTHAL

21 years ago

Footsteps clatter across the stone floor, drawing my gaze up. Narrowed eyes lock onto mine, and the familiar scent of fear fills the air. The creature bows low, trembling, words stuttering, "M–m–my king, I need y–your attention on the border of the Geheimnis Forest. Th-there is something you must see."

I rise, following the wretch. He is so thin his tattered robes slip from his shoulders; pants are tied three times to stay up. An embarrassment to my kingdom. His polished obsidian horns curl around his head, dark hair straggling in limp curls. Twainborn—half creature, half mortal. A reminder of the fragile alliance holding my kingdom together.

Take him, be rid of him, my shadows growl.

We tread through shadowy alleys, the obsidian stones cold beneath our feet. A flicker of blue, umber light dances ahead, guiding us toward the Geheimnis, the dark forest. Guards bow as I sweep past, hands on their blades, silencing my constant companion. Yet unease stirs. Its voice trembles and eyes plead, indicating this is no minor distraction.

The streets bend before me. My subjects lower their heads, shrinking from my presence. Fear clings to the air, metallic and sharp. My shadow drinks it in, begging release. *Please.* I indulge in them. Tendrils lash across the cobblestones, wringing screams from those who cower. Their terror fills me like wine. *Yes, I make them afraid.*

The twainborn stops at the edge of the forest, hand trembling as he points. There, just past the edge of the forest, a baby lies swirling in the shadows. They cover her like a blanket. Keeping her safe from the chill air of the Darklands.

Power, my shadows hum in my head.

Shadows writhe around her like a living cocoon, their tendrils twisting and pulsing with unnatural life. Soft cries hardly register as a pure, defiant light pulses within her. Bright green eyes blink up at me, fists clench, her skin is pale as moonlight.

The power radiates from her, and it is intoxicating. Everything in me longs to crush her into the earth, to silence that light, yet I steady my hand. This is no accident; this is a gift.

"Pick her up," I order. My voice cracks like a whip. "Take her to the castle. No one speaks of this."

The child's glow burns against the shadows that cling to her. Power hums against my bones, whispering of strength untold. *Take. Take.* A shiver runs through me. Her power will be mine. I will rip it from her body; I will manipulate it into something more. To take back what the gods have stolen from me.

Days pass. The child is tended to in my halls, swaddled in crimson silk and placed in an obsidian cradle. Even from across the throne room, her presence calls to me, in a low hum in the air, vibrating against my skin. *Ours.* My fingers twitch with the urge to seize it.

When the Seer arrives, a hush falls. Cloaked in black, her golden eyes gleam, too bright, too knowing. Those eyes, the ones I remember from before, but the gem at her throat unnerves me, not her gaze.

An emerald is strung on a silver chain. Its fire pulses like a heartbeat, alive, watchful. And its color ... the exact shade of the child's eyes.

My jaw clenches, my teeth grind together as I look at the emerald necklace. The urge to rip it off, to take this gem that took her from me, is overwhelming. The pounding of its power matches the baby. "It is a mirror of the child's eyes," I seethe, holding my hand back.

The Seer touches the stone, her fingers lingering with reverence. A flash of remembrance of the way her hand once lingered on my face. A faint smile curves her lips, a secret I cannot pry loose. "It mirrors nothing, my king. It remembers."

Her words burrow into me like a worm. I hate them. I hate her calmness. And yet I cannot look away from the gem, cannot ignore the way it seems to thrum in rhythm with the child's shallow breaths.

"There is much power in this room," she murmurs, her voice like shifting sand. "And you believe it belongs to you."

"Yes. The gods owe me something, for taking everything from me!" I yell, fury wrapping around me like a noose.

"Oh?" she cut me off, words flat and sharp. "Is that what you believe?"

Her golden eyes pierce me, stirring doubt I despise. Have the gods gifted her to me? Or is this a test? My jaw clenches. The baby whimpers in my arms; those cursed emerald eyes catch the torchlight, reflecting the Seer's gem.

The Seer's voice, cold as a winter wind, slices through the air as she lists her demands. A silver knife gleams in her hand in the dim light, reflecting her unreadable face. Special runes cover the blade, similar to the ones that cover the wall of the dungeon, that hide within the moss. Each one a symbol for the magic she possesses. She is not as I once remembered.

The pungent scent of herbs fills my nostrils, mingling with the smoky smell of impending doom. I feel the tremor of her gaze as I gather the black candles, each a silent testament to the ritual. Though I obey, rage boils in my chest, a searing heat threatening to consume me.

The throne room is cloaked in shadows, the only light emanating from the flickering candlelight that dances around the cradle. The air is still, with a faint scent of wax. The Seer's eyes burn gold as she lights the last flame. She beckons me, slicing my hand. Blood spills into the circle. Then she cuts the baby's foot, crimson dripping as the baby screams.

"Shhh... sweet Skia," she whispers.

My head snaps up. "What did you just call her?" a name that we use to speak about. A name for a different child. Our child.

The Seer only smiles, chanting in a tongue I do not know. Her golden eyes turn black. Shadows swell, twisting like a tornado, wind circling the room, and the child's glow tears free, rising into the air like a burning star.

Pain ignites in my chest as the light plunges into me. Fire consumes me from within, every vein aflame, my roar shakes the stones. Power courses through my body, a light penetrating the center of my chest, raw and unrestrained, until at last I crash to the floor.

When I rise, I am remade. Alive as I have not felt in centuries. A god among mortals. The world, once a canvas of muted grays, now explodes in a symphony of vibrant hues. *Yes*, my shadows purr. Their strength grows with each breath I take of my new power.

"She is bound to you now," the Seer declares. "Raise her as your own, or the power will vanish."

The words coil around me like chains. A mixture of rage and awe coats my throat. "She is not mine to raise," I affirm. Her eyes pierce my soul. It is a command, not a question. My hand brushes the silver crown upon my head—strange, heavy, yet thrumming with stolen light.

For a flicker, I think I see fear cross the Seer's face. Fear of me.

FOUR
SKIA

The scratching at my window snaps me awake.

Water sloshes up the sides of the tub, spilling onto the cold stone floor as I jolt upright. My skin prickles, breath comes shallow and fast. How long have I been asleep? The bathwater is icy now, my fingers pale and wrinkled, my body trembles from more than the cold.

The moonlight spilling through the glass was faint, fractured, and every shadow in the chamber seemed to spring to life.

Wrapping a cloth around myself, I creep across the slick floor. Again, the scratching comes, a slow, deliberate sound that seems to taunt me. The darkness presses in, heavy and thick. I hold my breath, straining to pinpoint the source. It seems to emanate from the far end of the hall, a rhythm that echoes in my chest. Each scrape is a whispered threat, a promise of what waits in the shadows.

The shadows within me stir, curling up my spine like smoke. *Let us out*, they purr. *Let us show you what claws sound like. Let us taste what awaits outside.* It feels like a piercing, unwelcome intrusion trying to breach the barriers of my mind. Their hunger sharpens my pulse.

I edge closer, heart hammering, each step loud against the silence. Another scrape against glass. My throat locks. My fingers hover over the latch.

A cat with black fur and orange eyes perches on the sill, as though mocking my fear.

Relief leaves me weak. My shoulders slump, breath rushes out in a half-laugh, half-sob. "Raven," I whisper, and push the window open.

She hops inside, tail curling, her body a ripple of shadow and grace. The moment her paws touch stone, her shape unravels, stretching upward, skin replacing fur until she stands before me again. Her grin is too sharp for a girl, and her eyes are still gleaming orange as she stands, tall and graceful.

I roll my eyes, though my smile trembles. "Why do you always do this? Sneak in like some thief."

"Because you always let me," she purrs, already sprawled across my bed as if she owns it.

By the time I dry my hair and pull on a robe, she lounges against the pillows, feline even in human form. I drop beside her, exhausted, trying to let her presence anchor me.

"My best friend," I mutter, tugging at her braid. "And the biggest menace alive."

Her canines flash when she grins. "What can I say, Skia? I had a feeling you needed company."

I swallow hard, the images from the dungeon still raw, burning at the edges of my thoughts. My father's secrets press heavy on me—the chains, the runes, the creature that screamed. My voice cracked when I whisper, "Distract me. Please. Tonight has been…" I couldn't even finish. "Just distract me."

Her eyes glow hotter, amused. "Then you'll like this. Someone from the Light Lands crossed the border."

I sat bolt upright. "That hasn't happened in hundreds of years."

The border was untouchable. Cursed by the gods. Guarded by Hunters who killed without hesitation. All my life I was told mortals and magicals must never meet, never taint the divide that keeps us alive.

"How?" I breathe. My mind is overflowing with possibilities. "How could they have gotten through the Geheimnis Forest?"

See, it begins. My shadows wake, intrigued.

Raven stretches like a cat waking from a nap, satisfaction curls her lips. "The king sent Hunters already. They'll make the fool suffer." Her tone is smooth, almost gleeful. My stomach knots.

I shiver. The Geheimnis Forest, a silent graveyard, offers no path. Soul-thieves and shadow-beasts prowl its endless dark. For someone to cross it... why? For what?

Raven tilts her head, orange eyes gleaming. "At least the Hunters finally have something useful to do. Hunting mortals. Killing them. Balance restored."

Her voice is too pleased. Her words slide like ice across my skin.

"What could a mortal possibly want from us?" I whisper, more to myself than her. There is no response, just

Raven's grin flickering in the firelight, and my shadows stir restlessly, disturbed by the silence.

FIVE
KING MORTHAL

7 years ago

The giggles of two girls, Skia and Raven, ricochet through the corridors, a shrill intrusion into the tranquil stillness of my throne room. Their laughter grates like broken glass against polished stone, shattering the silence I demand, the silence my kingdom knows to keep. The sound digs into my skull, each peal a claw raking across bone.

The caretaker is with them, that sniveling fool who had softened Skia. My Skia. His voice carries, warm, coaxing, drawing out her joy as though she were some mortal child playing in the markets instead of my heir. Every time she laughs, it rings with weakness. Fragility. He has nurtured something dangerous in her. He has ignited the light that I stole away.

My temples throb even though the room is dark. I close my eyes and inhale, letting my shadows curl free from beneath the throne. They slither across the floor, restless, whispering, *End him. Silence them. Take what is ours. Power.* The ache behind my eyes pulses in time with their hisses.

I want power; I want my people to beg at my feet for mercy. They brought the cruelty upon themselves.

Pushing my shadows out, they slam the door shut, blocking out the noise. Blessed silence swallows the air. I lean forward, nails biting into the scarred wood of the armrests until splinters break free. The shadows pound in my head. They feed upon the light that crowns my head. The light grants me immense power and control, intoxicating. However, it is not mine. A ticking time clock. *Tick, tick.*

Raven is another stray. Someone dumped her at my gate. They dragged her from the woods, a forgotten offering. Her mother tried to escape my power. She joined the resistance. They thought I was too dark and controlling. *They knew nothing.*

The mother didn't see the darkness in her daughter. They never do. The mother ran until the trees turned on her. The roots of my kingdom were stained by her blood. Her death didn't please me. Her failure did. It meant Skia now had a companion. A shadow. A mirror. Someone to bring out her shadows.

Yes, my shadows begged.

I should have discarded her as well, yet the moment I saw her eyes, burning orange, too sharp for a child, I knew she would serve a purpose.

Skia latched onto her. Of course, she did. Children cling to what mirrors them, even when that mirror is cracked and jagged. Skia thought Raven her playmate, her comfort, her rebellion against me. But I saw more. I saw the truth.

Raven is not like other children. Her darkness was not inherited but hammered into her soul by the taste of blood and the echoes of grief, even before she had learned to form words. Wildness wove itself into the very fabric of her being, manifesting in a girl's form. She chuckled, finding herself smiling when tears should have flowed. Servants whispered of finding her crouched by the stables, speaking to carcasses left for the hounds, as if she were conversing with their spirits. From the shadows, I witnessed her, her eyes alight with an unsettling interest, as she detached the wings, the crow's screams echoing in the stillness, her humming a chilling soundtrack.

Chaos disguised as innocence.

Skia did not see it. She saw only companionship. But I knew Raven was a seed, planted deep in Skia's life, destined to spread like a disease. My daughter still embraced a small flicker of innocence, a foolish, gentle glow. Raven would burn it out of her, and together they would burn for me. Scorching this world of all. The Light Lands would dry, the mortals dead.

Already the signs grew. Skia, once reluctant to use her shadows, now let them slip more easily when Raven is nearby. They whisper louder when the girls play together. Raven's laughter always feeds them.

The thought almost pleases me. Why should I waste my hand shaping Skia into what I need, when Raven will do it for me? One day, Skia's bond to that creature will tighten into a noose. And when it does, she will not escape.

I lean back into my throne, shadows pooling at my feet, purring like sated beasts. They feed off my power, grow with the light that I have stolen.

Yes, let her laugh for now. Let her believe in friendship. The echo of that laughter will eventually fade, replaced by screams, and the girl beside her will be responsible.

SIX
MEIR

The desert air is sharp and dry, stinging my eyes as I cross the coarse tan sands toward the lake. With every breath, the heat burns my nose. Each step raises dust that swirls around my legs, clinging to my boots. Ahead, the forest glimmers across the water, green and alive, mocking the parched barrenness of the Light Lands.

This lake is our lifeline, our only water source, and it is cursed. Shadows are sighted seeping from its depths more than ever before. My father fears conspiracy. Our council fears collapse. The people fear thirst.

I fear all of it.

I look to the sky and not a cloud grants coverage from the blasting heat. The irony of the Darklands flourishing while we mortals lack a drop of water. Though the skies threaten, we've never been granted a moment free of light. The few clouds coat the sky, but water never falls on my lands. The heat just rages, wreaking havoc on our crops, our homes, and my people.

The healers try. Once defenders of the realm, they are little more than keepers of our wells. Their light burns away the corruption from the water, but their strength wanes. Fewer are born with each generation. They are supposed to be our shield, yet now they barely keep us alive. A kingdom of light is powerless against the dark.

I—the prince of Luminaria—am expected to stand between my people and destruction. I am not ready. No matter how many hours I study, how often I follow my father as he teaches me, or how much my tutor yells to remember the important things, all I want is to be sparing in the training yards.

The weight presses into my chest with every breath, every step toward the lake. I have been raised to study, to train, to prepare, but none of that prepares me for this, the steady unraveling of the world around us.

My pace falters as I look at the sky ahead of me. Clouds gather over the mountains, dark and swollen, as storms tear across the border. My stomach lurches into my throat as I witness something terrible happening before my eyes. I sprint toward the lake, my mind overflowing with thoughts. By the time I reach the lake, the surface is no longer water. It darkens, swirling with pitch-black shadows. Black liquid night rolls and twists. The air smells of death and decay.

The darkness reaches for me, cold fingers brushing across my skin. My breath catches, but it passes me by, hungry for something more. The ground shudders. The sky dims. And then the world breaks.

Shadows pour from the lake, flooding outward, crawling into streets and homes. They rise into grotesque shapes, creatures of bone, and tear apart everything they touch.

I run. My sword weighs heavy in my hand, but it is nothing compared to the weight in my chest. I can no longer feel my feet. Each stomp echoes in my body as I race toward my home.

My people.

My father.

The castle rises in the distance, crystal spires catching the last of the light. Our beacon. Our hope. And before my eyes, it darkens. Shadows claw their way up the walls, blackening the crystal, devouring its brilliance. My scream tears free, but the sound is lost in the chaos.

Night falls where night should not exist.

The market collapses in panic. Merchants abandon their stalls, families scatter, guards shout and die. Shadows rip into the crowd, dragging bodies into the dark. I force my legs to move faster, though every muscle screams and fights as I push forward. Demanding the guards to do something, anything to stop the advances on my kingdom. I have to reach the castle.

But I am too late.

The darkness swallows it whole. As if liquid, the darkness seeps, and oozes down the sides. With sharp claws ripping into the impenetrable walls, the creature climbs the castle's side.

A sob escapes my lips. The ground buckles. I collapse, landing hard on my hands and knees. The ground scorches my palms.

No, not the ground.

Pain explodes through my chest. I scream as fire burns through my body. What is happening to me? My scream is ripped apart by light—light pours from me, flooding my hands, my chest, my very skin. It blinds the world, burns the shadows, sears them away in a flood of gold.

And then, silence.

The sun breaks through again. The shadows vanish. But the land is ruined. Streets littered with bodies, pools of blood darken against stone. Survivors stumble out of hiding; their grief is a sound I will never forget.

And my hands still glow.

I stare at them in horror. A memory flashes behind my eyes. Blinding my ability to see anything else. One I was forced to forget. A memory stolen from my childhood flickers with gold, moments of impossible instinct, all stolen from my memories. until now, the light awakening something in me I had forgotten. Now it roars in me, undeniable. The shock staggers through my body.

I am mortal; this is wrong.

Everything is wrong.

The shadows vanish, but their damage, but their damage lingers, the buildings in ruin, the carts of the marketplace scatter the streets.

The shock reverberates through my body.

I stumble toward the castle, my heart demanding only one answer. My father. He has to live.

The guards meet me at the gates, their faces pale. "Prince Meir—the king…" The words falter.

Inside, crystal halls glitter with fractured light. Prisms broken. Walls cracked. Every step carries me closer to dread. Kain waits—my friend, my brother in all but blood. His hand grips my shoulder, steady, though his eyes tell me everything.

"Is he alive?" I whisper.

"He breathes," Kain says. "But a curse grips him. Shadows coil through his veins. The healers failed. Only one … perhaps…might have the power to try. We wait." His words cut off.

My rage breaks. "Then bring them faster! This is the king!" My entire body shakes as the words and spit leave my mouth. This is not acceptable; he is king! I storm to his quarters, the sound echoing through the hall, my rage leaving behind whispers of fear to the staff.

Kain holds me back at the door, his voice low, weighted. "Meir. Are you prepared to see him like this?"

I cannot answer. I nod anyway.

Inside, the air is heavy. Such darkness in such a bright place. My father lies still, shadows vein his body, black spreads across his lips. His chest rises shallowly. He is alive. And he is lost.

I sink beside him, pressing my head to the bed. I grab his hand, and it is cold to the touch. He is always warm. The kingdom will fall. And I, unready, unwilling, will be king.

The light inside me will not be silenced.

It bursts again, golden fire searing my veins, pouring from my palms into his broken body. I beg it to be enough. Beg the gods. Beg anyone.

When it fades, nothing has changed. His body remains bound in darkness.

And I am left with the truth.

The shadows have won.

My father is gone. Even as his breath rises in his chest.

SEVEN
KING MORTHAL

6 years ago

The feet of Skia and Raven patter against the forest floor as I stand at the edge of the Whispering Woods. They haunt just along the edge of the Geheimnis Forest, encouraging their shadows but do not take them fully, it is the border of our lands.

The air hangs heavy with damp earth and rotting leaves, the familiar perfume of decay. It both comforts and chills me. For years, I have watched this child grow, her shadow powers the only constant in her life. Like a phantom, she dances in the gloom, dark tendrils curling from her fingers, a sharp contrast to the innocence etched on her small face.

And always, she struggles. The shadows whisper to her as they still whisper to me. They want to devour her spirit, twist her heart into something cruel. She is light —for all her darkness—laughter that rings like bells, curiosity that defies the filth of the Shadowlands. I should crush it. I should hate her.

But I don't.

The silver crown gleams and pulses against my black hair, a reminder of what I am, what I have stolen, and yet even I cannot deny the bond that chains me to her. I want to despise her, this living weapon that the gods have thrust into my hands. But in her eyes, I see something familiar. A reflection I cannot bear.

It is treachery ... this ... connection. So, I sharpen it until it is something useful. If I cannot hate her, then I will use her. I will mold her into a blade, strip away her joy and leave only shadow. Her innocence has lasted too long, she is far past childhood. I will burn it from her until she has no one left but me.

The first step is obvious. I sever her ties. She clings too much to that creature—Ashmore. They make their way back to the castle. His laughter is sunlight, a poison to the rot I have meticulously sown. His affection, his unyielding presence—it has to be destroyed. He would be replaced by Raven.

As the plan crystallizes in my mind, I turn away from the edge of the Whispering Woods, the damp air clinging to my cloak like a second skin. The rain hangs in the air constantly. The forest seems to recoil from me, branches bending back as I pass, wary of the darkness I command. Skia's laughter still echoes faintly behind me, swallowed by the gloom. I stride through the tangled undergrowth, boots silent on moss and fallen leaves, my thoughts as sharp as the crown upon my brow.

The trees thin, giving way to the cobbled path that leads to the castle. Shadows trail me, eager for the task ahead, whispering promises of ruin. The walls of the castle rise before me, cold and resolute, banners limp in the windless haze. Guards stand aside, eyes cast downward, sensing the chill that follows in my wake.

Following the laughter, I ascend the stone steps, crossing the threshold into the grand hall. The space looms vast and empty, every torch casting long, wavering shadows across polished marble. There, Ashmore awaits, unaware of the pain he will soon endure. Skia lingers at his side, her innocence glowing faintly amid the encroaching darkness. The time has come to sever what binds her to the light. To rip away the last warmth she knows and reshape her with shadow.

The grand hall rang with my command. "Ashmore. Take Skia to her room. Then meet me below the throne room."

The old fool's shoulders sag, though his brown eyes burn with recognition. He knows. His fear is delicious. Skia's head tilts up at him, confusion clouding her features. She doesn't know yet that I am about to cut out the last scrap of warmth she has clung to.

That was the point.

Below the throne room, I stand waiting for Ashmore to appear. My feet pacing across the dark stone floor. The air is chilled, a small wind cutting through the hall, the blue umberflame flickering making the shadows play against the wall.

I hear his hooves clomp against the floor. He does not slow his pace, he walks defeated, his head hanging down and tears shining behind his eyes. My hand grabs the door handle and turns. The earthy smell slams me in the face.

The dungeon door slams shut behind us, shadows flickering eagerly in the corners. My shadows hiss and writhe, restless for blood. They know what is coming. The air thickens with the promise of violence.

Ashmore follows me slowly. His once jovial face is drawn and pale. Every step weighs with grief. His eyes meet mine, red-rimmed with sleeplessness, and for a heartbeat I almost see the courage he once had. But it is gone now. He clutches his tunic like a man trying to hold himself together. No bravery found, not a trace on his face. He is giving up, allowing the darkness to win.

"Why?" His voice cracks. "Why take me from the child?"

I almost laugh at the desperation in his tone. Almost. Instead, I let the silence draw out until the weight of it presses against him.

"Because she needs no one. You will soften her. You will destroy her." My words cut through the hall like steel.

And then my shadows are on him. They tear him apart in a tide of black, dragging him down, breaking his bones one by one. His screams ring against the stone, a symphony that rattles the torches. Their flames dance wildly, shadows mocking his agony in grotesque shapes.

I crouch, hand under his chin, forcing his tear-streaked face to meet mine. "This will hurt," I whisper, smiling as the last of his strength falters.

"Bring me Skia," I bark to the guards lining the dungeon.

Chains biting deep into his wrists. The air reeked of rot, of damp stone and despair. The iron door groans open again, and small footsteps echo down the stairs.

Skia appears down at the bottom of the stairway, she stops, the sight stopping her in her tracks. Her expression dropping as her eyes roam the room.

Her wide eyes lock on him—this broken, bloodied man who had once been her comfort, her shield. Anguish cracks across her features, her young face too small to hold so much pain. It is cruel. Making her take the life of someone who spent his life flourishing hers. In the questions that coat her face, I see the anguish; I can feel her need to flee. I reach out with my shadows, holding her in place, and come up behind her.

"Kill him," I order, my voice echoing against the walls. My shadows ripple at her feet, eager, waiting. I can see her shaking, the sweat beading on her hairline.

"Why?" She questions her voice cracking.

Ashmore's gaze finds hers. Not mine. Hers. Even as the chains cut him open, even as blood drips to the floor, he seeks only her face. It is not fear in his eyes anymore, but sorrow. And love.

Enough.

I lean close to her ear, letting the shadows curl around us both. "Feed them, Skia. Let your shadows take him. Only then will they obey you."

"I cannot." Her lip trembles. Her fists clench.

"You must." I demand.

The torches sputter. The dungeon seems to hold its breath. And Ashmore, poor, pathetic, ruined, loyal Ashmore, closes his eyes, as if in some irrevocable act of mercy, so she cannot see the life leave his eyes. His final mercy, because he knows I will give her no choice. Not anymore.

It is the beginning of her unraveling. And the first thread of the weapon I would forge her into.

EIGHT
SKIA

The dream comes back, as it always does. Darkness pressing around me, thick and suffocating, carrying the damp scent of stone and the metallic tang of blood.

Ashmore lies on the dungeon floor, broken. My shadows have torn him apart, leaving his body twisted, oozing black ichor. His blood. My doing.

Behind me stands my father, silent, immovable, his gaze sharp enough to cut me in two. His shadows freeze me as surely as chains. The shadows inside me writhe and push, eager for release, their whispers drowning out my own thoughts.

I remember the moment I gave in. The shadows poured from me, a black tide that wrapped around Ashmore, dragging breath from his lungs. Ashmore, my mentor, my protector, the man who had raised me with gentleness my father never gave, looks up at me. His eyes, once warm with laughter, shine with pain. They plead. Not for life, but for release.

"He is not worthy of this life, Skia," my father's voice rasps, low and cruel. "End it."

By not speaking up for him, I am complicit in his death.

I raise my hands. The shadows obey. His gasps choke into silence as they fill him, smother him, break him. His body stiffens on the stone, and my hands, my shadows, are the cause. The weight of his death would never leave me, and the little pieces he had put together lay broken amongst his body on the cold stone floor.

I wake gasping, tangled in sheets, hair damp with sweat, tears burning my eyes. The dream never changes. And the guilt never fades.

That day I understood my father for what he was. A man who would make me his weapon. And I saw what he wanted me to become. A tool of darkness. But buried deep inside, even then, was something else. A spark of defiance. A whisper of hope that he would not own me forever.

I pull myself out of bed before the nightmare can drag me under again. The shadows snicker at the edges of my thoughts, feeding on my fear. But I push them back as I put on my clothes and leave the castle.

My feet land in a puddle as I step out of the secret tunnel. Raven and I have used this tunnel on many occasions to get away from the darkness of the castle. Another puddle as I continue down the back ally that leads to the market. My hood covers my head, my eye looking to the ground trying to remain unnoticed. Most of my features can become a curtain of disguise but the green eyes are always a giveaway to my true identity. The Princess of Shadows.

The market is rife with rumors. The attack on Luminaria. Their king is near death, by shadows. Our shadows. Voices carry the news in hurried, fearful tones, but nothing they say matches what I had seen with my own eyes in the dungeon. No remarks of a shadow creature, vile and deadly, attacking the Light Lands. They remain ignorant of the full story. And I need to find out the truth.

I keep walking, though every step feels heavier. War comes. War breaks both kingdoms, and my silence is part of the cause. I hate myself for it.

A flash of movement catches my eye, a shadow fox darting in and out of the alleys, sleek and playful, a spark of innocence in a land drowning in darkness. My shadows whisper at once; *blood is already on your hands.*

They are right.

The Shadowlands aren't evil. My father is. His cruelty has poisoned everything, twisting shadows darker, teaching people to fear and betray. Yet still, life clings here—foxes darting, ravens cawing from rooftops, dragons sweeping in the dark gray sky.

The moons cast shadows on the gothic buildings that line the streets. A variety of goods overflows the carts that line the edges of the cobblestone streets. The merchants lose themselves in gossip with one another or in trying to sell their goods to each person who walks by. Umberflames flicker blue firelight in lanterns, casting a ghostly light along the cobblestones, tinting the area blue. For a moment, I want to believe in our magic, in the beauty of our lands. Only for a moment.

Ahead, the vampires' lair looms atop a hill. It rises above all the other sections of our city. The vampires are the wealthiest of all the creatures of my land. Having control of most of our government. Riven, the wealthiest of them all, is known for his unkind deeds. He wreaks havoc on all that dares to question the laws of this land. He and my father are close, Riven seeing him as an idol, and he actively pursues me to reach his ultimate power.

He has a way with words that I often believed meant change. But he always stays the same. A constant truth that haunts my presence. A weakness that I too often allow to break me. My body wanders closer, its needs, simple oblivion is the only gift he gives me. Vampires have a strong psychotropic component in their fangs that allow their victims to experience ecstasy as they draw blood.

At the end of the path to the vampire's lair two vampires lean against the gate. Gates that keep any unwanted visitors out. Their eyes catch mine. A nervous flip in my stomach betrays the fact that I know one of them. Silver hair, bright red eyes. Riven smiles, fangs flashing sharp against his lips. He looks like temptation made flesh. He is elegant, predatory, beautiful in a way that makes my stomach clench with both disgust and want.

His stare pins me in place, dredging up memories of his teeth at my throat, the shiver of ecstasy and horror that follows. My shadows stir, restless. I force myself to keep walking, telling myself I don't need this. I don't need him..

His voice slides into my mind, smooth and mocking. "Ski. Just a little bite. It's been weeks."

I clench my fists. "Stay out of my head, Riven."

He only laughs. "I've barely begun."

He walks toward me, his hand sliding into his loose slacks. His stomach is bare, chiseled as marble. His skin pale beneath the shadows that curve along his abs. He wears a black jacket, gold embroidery along the edges. He holds it back to show off more of his chest. My eyes break to his, cutting myself off from the lingering stare. He smirks, his other hand raising to rub against his sharp jaw.

He stops in front of me, pulls me forward against his body and bends down to whisper in my ear. "Just let me have a small taste of you, let me taste your shadows."

My body moves back, my eyes meeting his. He knows every weakness, he seeks control, just like my father.

I know I need to leave, even so, I follow him. Not because I want him. But because I want nothing. No thoughts. No weight. The ecstasy that pounds behind his fangs. For the shadows to stop haunting me with their voices. Just silence.

Leaving the chaos of the streets, I trail behind him up the stairs to his manor, away from the noise.

Are you sure we can trust this one? The shadows question. Riven is the leader of the ward, royalty. He is not someone I want to spend my life with, yet he is my betrothed. He is a distraction. A distraction from every thought that spirals in my mind.

He leads me by the hand, glancing back, his fangs visible from the small gap of his lips. His guards nod as we enter through the large black doors. As I walk in, I am greeted by the familiarity. The foyer walls are coated in red, the blue umber light burning from the silver chandelier making it a violet red. I follow him to the grand room, and the room is filled with proof of his power. Gold objects, collectibles that come from the gods. The walls are covered with gothic paintings. Haunting figures etched on canvases. Others are here, vampires enjoying their prey in the hidden corners of the room though none turn to look as we pass. We find a dark corner hidden behind the shadows in the room.

"What bothers you, Skia? Shadows troubling you again?" he asks his voice low.

"I am not here for conversation, Riven."

He wraps me in an embrace, his cool body chilling me. "What are you after tonight dear? My body or my fangs?" he says his voice vibrating my ears, a warmth building in my stomach. I have come to this manor too often, a terrible relationship. A relationship built on need and control.

"Just your fangs, Riven." I say, shame building in my core.

He eyes the red velvet couch. "Sit." he commands. His body is still close, making my body react is a deceiving way.

I sit on the couch, and I maintain eye contact.

"Lie down," he orders and I do as he says. My eyes never break with his as he walks across the room toward me, his pale skin looking almost white under the umber light, his mouth is violet. I watch as his tongue runs along his fangs, a deeper desire trying to break through.

He stops in front of me, dropping to one knee. His hands grabbing my face firmly, turning my head exposing my neck. I feel his body against mine, and my heart is pounding in my throat. His fangs sink into me, sharp and merciless. Pain and pleasure intertwine until I can't separate them. My tears burn, but do not fall, before the venom mixes with my blood. My thoughts sink away, the sound of my blood flowing in his mouth taking over any thought that tries to break through my brain. Every limb feels heavy, but my mind feels as if it's floating. A million stars radiate behind my eyes, and a sigh escapes my mouth. His hands touching my stomach, his desires taking over his body. My mind is no more of this world or another, it is a state of oblivion. A moan escapes my throat as the sensation takes over. His mouth breaking away, his tongue trailing up my throat. He licks off every drop of blood. When he finishes, he looks at me, wipes his mouth.

"If you have a craving for anything else just let me know." he leaves me there, empty and ashamed. Shadows whisper their triumph. As soon as I can manage to get up without falling over, I stumble out of his manor, back into the streets, convincing myself I am fine. But nothing about me is fine.

Tripping over stones, I feel the spots on my neck disappear. For now, my mind is empty, the blood loss making my head feel foggy. The forest rises in the distance; its edge is a black line of menace. Its monsters keep us trapped, prisoners in our own land.

Turning down the cobblestone street. I see the Blackrock Pub in the distance. It is falling apart, the sign hanging by one chain, blowing back and forth in the wind. The pub is crowded tonight, I can barely hear my thoughts as I make my way through. It is packed with shapeshifters, vampires, and witches indulging in mischief. They celebrate Luminaria's fall, toasting to war. Their cheers make me sick. The bartender looks at me, his shadows stirring. He probably works for my father, keeping track of me, not allowing me to leave the Shadowlands. Their desire to keep me here only ignites my desire to leave even more.

The strong smell of ale fills my nose as I round the bar, finding the barmaid. Her face is beautiful. Her eyes are a shade of violet, that almost look black. Sandy blond hair falls to her waist.

She leans over, resting on her elbows, and asks. "What can I get you?"

"Same as always," I answer. This pub is like a second home, a place where people ask no questions.

I scan the room until I find her, a sleek black cat perched on a stool, orange eyes glinting in the firelight. Raven. My only confidant. My only friend. The only person in this entire land I can trust.

Grabbing my mug I walk over to Raven. I scratch behind her ears, whispering, "Too crowded. Let's go." She chirps in agreement and shifts into herself, tall and lean, eyes sparkling in the dim.

Together, we slip through the crowd and out into the quiet night.

"Not celebrating tonight, Ski?" Raven tilts her head, studying me as though she already knows the answer.

She always knows. She's the only one I can tell the truth to. The only one who lives through her own darkness, who understands mine. Understands the darkness of my shadows and the weight that they make me carry.

Her smile turns sharp. "I wish I'd seen the Light King's face when the shadows came."

A chill prickles down my spine. She means it. She wants it. And, gods help me, a part of me does too.

NINE
SKIA

Raven found me in the library searching through the countless books trying to find a connection to the runes that hide in the dungeon and the one that marks my hand. It is hidden, a faint scar that catches in the blue umberlight. I hear her come up behind me as I flip the pages.

"What are you doing, Skia?" Raven purrs. She knows I am not allowed to be in the library, knows that my father forbids it. He wants to limit everything, keeping secrets. Every chance I get is spent sneaking here, reading the pages and growing my knowledge of my world.

"I was just looking for something." I reply. I know I can trust her, she is my best friend, but something in me whispers to tell a lie.

"Lets go have some fun." She says, closing the book and grabbing my hand.

The torchlight flickers against the stone as Raven and I slip down one of the castle's back corridors. Our laughter echoes too loudly in the quiet halls. My shadows cling close, hissing at me to be cautious, but I ignore them. Tonight isn't about caution. Tonight is about pretending that I am just a girl sneaking out with her best friend.

"You're walking too loudly," I whisper, pressing a hand to her arm.

Raven rolls her bright orange eyes, the slit pupils catching the glow like embers. "You're just paranoid, Ski. No one's awake at this hour except your father's pet guards, and half of them would fall asleep if you snapped your fingers."

Her grin is sharp, mischievous. She makes everything feel lighter, even in this fortress of cold stone and secrets. With her, the weight of power, of what I would become, slips away for a little while.

We duck into the old training yard, long since abandoned, its sparring dummies fraying and tilting in the moons light. The air smells of dust and old sweat, but here, surrounded by shadows and silence, I could breathe. The moons glare as if they are watching us find trouble.

"Come on," Raven urges, tossing me a practice blade from the rack. Her grin widens, fangs just showing. "Let's see if you're still as terrible as the last time."

I groan as I catch the blade. "One of these days, I'm going to beat you."

Let us out and you will. The shadows purr in my ear, always wanting to be released, wanting to take.

She prowls forward, light on her feet, and lunges. Our blades clash, thudding against the air, in the quiet. Raven moves like water, like a cat, fast, fluid, merciless. I stumble more than I strike, laughing even as sweat drips down my back.

"You're hesitating," she says, circling me, her voice half-tease, half-lesson. "The shadows are in you, Ski. Stop fighting like a Lumi and use them."

"I don't want to use them," I snap, parrying one of her blows.

Her grin softens, almost sad. "Then you'll always fight with half of yourself tied down."

We spar until my arms ache and my legs tremble. When I finally collapse against the wall, she drops beside me with feline grace, her orange eyes glowing in the dim. She laughs, the sound bubbling out of her chest, and I can't help but laugh with her, despite the bruises I know I'll have tomorrow.

"You fight like a bird," she teases.

"And you fight like you're half-cat," I shoot back, shoving her shoulder.

"Maybe I am." Her smile lingers, but then it softens. She turns to me, brushing a curl of hair from my face. "You know you can tell me anything, right? Even the things you don't tell him."

The words strike deeper than I want them to. I nod, biting my lip. Raven is the only one who ever sees me—the real me, not the heir, not the weapon, not the shadow's child. Just Skia.

"I know," I whisper. "I don't know what I'd do without you."

She doesn't answer, but her hand squeezes mine.

"Wine?" she smirks, knowing the answer before she asks.

"Always," I say back. She gets up leaving me lying down in the grass looking up to the sky. It is filled with stars, The moons glow bright and the dragons fill the air with their wings flapping across the land.

As I wait for Raven to fetch a flask of stolen wine from the kitchens, I wander the yard, trailing my fingers along the cracked stones. My shadows stretch lazily, curling across the ground. For once, they feel content, almost quiet.

That's when I hear it, voices, low and urgent, slipping from the archway near the hall.

I freeze.

"...she trusts you," my father's voice, deep and cold, carries on the still air.

Raven's reply is softer, trembling at the edges. "She's my friend."

"She is your duty," Morthal corrects, his words like a blade sliding from its sheath. "You will remember that. When the time comes, you will do what is required."

A pause. My heart hammers.

And then Raven says, "I will do what I must."

The silence afterward is heavier than the words. My shadows fidget, tasting the lie, or the truth, in the air. In the hollow part of my stomach, doubt forms.

I step back, pressing into the wall until the stone bites into my spine. My breath comes shallow, my pulse a frantic drum. What did he mean? Why iss she speaking to him at all? She always speaks of how much she loathes my father ... but this...my thoughts float away, not wanting to find the answer to the questions that spiral in my head.

The shadows whisper suspicions, fanning the spark of fear. *Betrayal. Lies. We warned you.*

No. I shake my head, forcing the whispers away. This is Raven. My Raven. The girl who pulled me out of the library rafters when I fell, who bled beside me when we cut our palms and promised we'd always choose each other.

I can't doubt her. I won't.

When she returns, wine in hand and a wicked grin on her lips, I paste on a smile. She flops beside me, pressing the flask into my hands.

"See? Told you I wouldn't get caught."

I drink, the burn of the liquid distracting from the ache in my chest.

I laugh with her until dawn, but the words I had overheard carve themselves into me like runes on stone. I would not let myself believe them.

And yet... a seed of doubt is planted, and I cannot pull it free.

TEN
SKIA

The Seer is here. The thwack of her sandals echoes in the hall. Each step sounds like a purpose. There is an energy about her, a pull almost to me. She has been in and out of the castle since my childhood, my father exploiting her visions for his own greed.

Behind her fall silent footsteps, a slight drag of a cloak is all you hear. The Seer's second follows behind. Her name is Lucile, a vampire who is cursed with the sight.

The Seer are ancient beings, their abilities spanning power and prophecy. Their line repeating the history others didn't learn from.

The size of Seer didn't matter compared to the energy that radiates off of her. She has golden skin, that glows from within, like gold flakes dancing upon her skin. Her hair is midnight black, falling into waves that are hidden by a dark cloak. She wears an emerald against her chest that pulses like its own heartbeat, almost calling to me. Her golden eyes flicker in the light, each blink summoning more depth, the gold pulsing and shifting. They are heavy with the visions, yet her skin has not aged over the years that I have seen her. Her true age is unknown to me.

Each year my father calls for her. He says he seeks prophecy, but the look behind his eyes shows more. He has a fondness, a gentleness, when he sees her. One that infuriates him, because unlike all his followers, she does not fall for his deceit.

"Hello," she says to King Morthal.

"I have gathered an audience in the ballroom, and all are prepared to hear the prophecy." the guard says.

Each year she shows up with a prophecy that holds meaning to my kingdom, a large harvest for the season, an attack from an enemy, something that my father can act on. Building his power, giving him more control. I never understood her reasoning in giving him power.

"There is a light in you." Her fingers gripping my wrist and turning me. Her touch does not hurt. It is gentle. My eyes look into hers. A pulling feeling wraps around my core.

Light in me? The thought is unbearable. Shadows are all I have ever known. They fill my days with rage and pain, gnaw at my bones, and wrap around my soul like chains. Every breath feels heavy, as though I am drowning in an endless abyss. Despair clings to me, relentless, suffocating.

And yet... some fractured part of me yearns. Yearns for light, for even the smallest spark to pierce through the darkness that swallows me. But no matter how I reach for it, hope slips away like smoke.

I pull back from her and say, "There is no light in me, I am of darkness." I turn to walk away, her hand holds me in place.

Her eyes are glazed over, she is not of this world. Her body taken over by a vision, a reaction I have never seen until this moment. That all other prophecies have been a manipulation.

Lucile stands in the back, watching the words spew from her mouth.

"The sun will become dark. The day will become night. Two souls collide. One lost. One found. On the edge of rocks, darkness will become light." her voice is not of her own.

Her eyes are off in a faraway land. My eyebrows knit together, and I reach for her hand, squeezing it and saying her name. "Seer," I say. "We need to get to the ballroom." She nods her head yes, and she turns to leave. I follow behind. Her body flows with elegance as we make our way to the ballroom.

The room is filled with chairs that are occupied by all types of creatures of power that walk in the Dark Lands. The vampires sit up toward the front, Riven's eyes following me. I sit down on the opposite side of the aisle, ignoring his eyes. I watch Seer as she gracefully walks up the steps to the highest part of the room. Her cape rippling against the stairs.

She looks out to all and then she closes her eyes and speaks the words. "The Light King will bring light to all parts of the Shadowlands. He will command control over all the Shadowlands and cast all that do not follow the light out." She breaks off.

That is not the prophecy. She just declared war.

Lucile stands behind her, showing no emotion as she hears the lies fed to the crowd. In this moment I see the fabrication, her eyes catching mine, no clouds covering them. Clear.

A knot of fear surges from my gut, pressing against my throat. The roar of my shadows, a secret that angers them, fills my ears. My vision blurs and tunnels begin to close in on my vision. A wave of nausea has me grabbing the sides of my seat, seeking the cold stone I sit on. My shadows hiss in my ears.

Why would not she mention the prophecy that she spoke in the room? How many years has she been deceiving us with false prophecies that led us to this time, pushing us to war?

Her eyes watch me, her gaze burning hot, like words she can not say boil there. I feel hollow, and at this moment I feel as if she is telling me something more. The final reason a push out of the door.

As she descends, she lit the flame that will spark a war, that turns the day to night.

I have to go to the Light Lands. To Luminaria. Crossing the border means death, but perhaps his light holds the answers my shadows don't have. The healers in the mortal realm wield only faint echoes of light, just enough to cure sickness and mend wounds. True power has not stirred in Luminaria for generations. Their defenses barely hold against the creeping dark.

But if he bears the light the Seer speaks of, then he is the key. I must find him. If her words are true, then light lives within me. And that is the most dangerous secret of all.

ELEVEN
SKIA

Days pass, and the uneasiness grows within me. The mortal that crossed over the border has not been seen since. Rumors flood the streets with conspiracies. Talk of resistance and the leader behind it.

The wind whips through my hair as I sit perched on the jagged edge of the castle's highest tower. Lyra, my dragon, circles above. Her silver wings slicing through the night sky. The sound of her roar vibrates against the stone at my back. She is one thing father can't take away. Dragons are free, they roam across the lands and do not answer to the Shadowlands. Being chosen by a dragon is a sign of great power. My father was enraged the day a dragon bonded me. He was never chosen for the honor. While bonded, she is her own entity.

Each beat of her wings sends shadows spilling across the tower walls in fleeting, shifting shapes. Her silver wings stir the wind as she flies around the towers. I lean my head against the stone and breathe.

Here I am alone. Here, I can breathe.

From this height, the Shadowlands stretch in every direction, the rolling hills drown in indigo twilight, farmlands fall silent under the weight of eternal night, and the Geheimnis Forest looms just beyond the mountains, its tree lines a smear of black ink across the horizon. The Shadowlands are vast, alive, and suffocating.

Tonight, the heavens above are a tapestry of awe. Three moons hang suspended in the obsidian vault. One is colossal and bright. Its silver glow paints the castle walls in pale fire. One is crimson, bleeding faint light across the clouds, and one is blue, small and soft, like a secret only the night can keep. Their mingled light turns the kingdom ghostly and strange—beautiful even in its decay.

Dragons wheel above the mountains, their shadows sweep the peaks. They come and go as they please, the only creatures of the Shadowlands that can. Their cries roll like thunder, carrying wild hunger in the crisp air. This is their hour, their kingdom as much as ours. We live and die with them—strength and ruin bound in their wings.

I lean against the wall, stone biting into my back, and sigh. This place is my sanctuary. It towers beyond my father's reach, defying his control. But tonight, the weight in my chest refuses to ease. Whispers of war press closer with every rumor. Shadows grow restless beneath my skin. And the prophecy ... the prophecy gnawed at me until I could hardly stand still.

Watching the sky alive with flying creatures, my mind wanders. The Seer's voice claws at my memory.

Light in me? Impossible. I am darkness. There is no light within me. There is always a shadow. I kill with them, breathe with them, feel them as marrow in my bones. They curl now at my feet on the tower ledge, restless, aching for freedom, whispering dark promises. Darkness is all I know. And yet her words still haunt me.

The memory of Seer's eyes burned into mine, the golden pots hypnotizing me, unblinking, as if daring me to believe it. Daring me to question her, deny her false prophecy.

Lyra roars above, breaking me from my thoughts, sensing the storm that churns inside me. If only I could read her thoughts, as she could read mine. My thoughts flood her mind, but she is careful with any she allows me to hear. A connection, a threat to my happiness, because every time I am close to anyone or anything, he rips them from me. I press my hand to the stone, grounding myself, and whisper the plan that has been festering in my chest for days. She listens with gleaming violet eyes, her body tense, but she will fly when I call her.

I rise from the edge of the tower; the wind snatches the breath from my lungs and I climb down, sneaking into the window. I am on the other side of the castle. My shadows trail me down the hallways, whispering doubts, mocking my resolve. I keep moving.

In my chamber, I strip off my gown and pull-on black trousers and a tunic, slipping my cloak over my shoulders, the hood low to shroud my face. Each step toward the side door feels like a heartbeat too loud, like the castle itself might scream my betrayal. If my father catches me, he will kill me—twice if he must—and no crown, no bloodline, will save me.

But staying means silence.

And silence means war.

At the door, I slip into the night.

Raven finds me before I find her.

A sleek black cat trots out of the alley, chirping. Her tail flicks as she winds around my ankles before shifting in a shimmer of fur and bone. In her place stands my best friend, dark curls tumbling wild over her shoulders, orange-slit eyes glowing with mischief even in shadow.

"Hello, Raven," I whisper.

She links her arm through mine without hesitation, like we are two girls sneaking toward the market looking for trouble.

The square pulses with life. Shapeshifters hawking their tricks, vampires laughing too loudly in the corners, meat roasting over flames. Spells crackle from tent to tent, charms gleaming beneath lantern light. The atmosphere around us is alive and sparking with electricity. Smoke curling upward, mingling with the moonlight. The whispers conceal secrets in the shadows. For a heartbeat, the night feels almost ordinary.

But Raven knows me too well. She tugs me to a stop, her gaze sharp. "Skia, what is it? What's wrong?"

My throat closes. Tears prick hot. "Just ... everything," I whisper, voice breaking as she brushes a strand of hair from my cheek. She pulls me into her arms, holding me like she always has when the nights are too dark, when my father's shadows press too heavy.

We find a secluded corner, away from curious ears, and I tell her. The prophecy. The Seer's words. My plan is to leave the Shadowlands and cross into Luminaria.

Her face hardens; fangs flash behind her lips. "You cannot do this. If your father finds out, he'll gut you and hang you in the square. He does not care that you are his heir. He cares only about control." Her voice drops lower, edged with a growl. "This path will lead to your death, Skia. You know that."

"I know," the words crack inside me, but I hold her gaze. "But if I sit still—if I do nothing—war consumes us. My father never seeks peace. He wants destruction. He wants conquest. And if the prophecy is true...then I have to try. Even if it costs me everything." Everything has become too much, and the abuse that has haunted me for my entire life sparks the fire I need to leave. The secret that grows within me. Everything my father has done, broken me piece by piece, has shoved me out the door, instead of controlling me like he hopes.

The market blurs through my tears—laughter, shouts, children chasing sparks of magic. Innocents who suffer for my father's greed. My hand clenches Raven's. "They deserve better than this. They deserve a chance to choose their lives, Raven."

She shakes her head, torn between fury and fear, but she doesn't let go of me. Not once. Behind her eyes I see something more, but the words do not escape from her mouth.

I lean forward and press a kiss to her forehead, whispering against her skin. "I'll be okay. I promise."

The words taste like ash. For both of us, we know it is hollow.

But there is no going back. Not now.

TWELVE
MEIR

The sun blazes in my eyes as I step onto the sparring grounds, packed dirt crunching beneath my boots. Kain is already there, grinning, sword in hand.

"Ahh, my man—soon to be king!" he calls, tossing my blade toward me. I catch it, the weight familiar, grounding. "Come on, kingly. Surely little ol' me can't defeat you?"

His laughter rings across the yard as he lunges. Steel clashes, the impact reverberating up my arms. I brace, feet sliding into position, and strike back. Blow after blow, our swords crack against one another until sweat soaks my shirt and the sun climbs higher. Finally, I knock his weapon free, both of us breathless and grinning in the heat of it.

We collapse onto the grass. I drain my waterskin, cool liquid spilling down my chin, and lay back against the earth. A moment, no thoughts of the future or the darkness that awaits me in the castle. The sky stretches endlessly and blue above me, so different from the storm-laden horizon at the mountains' edge. The constant worry of what happens if the storms spread again, the anguish of my people, still trying to put the pieces back together.

"How is the king?" Kain asks quietly, settling beside me.

My chest tightens. "Worse. The darkness spreads every day. His face..." I swallow hard, pushing down the lump that threatens to overtake me in grief. "I barely recognize him now. The shadows crawl into his mouth, his eyes, his very veins. He breathes still, but only just." Reliving every broken breath, wondering when it will be his last. Seeing him in this state is agonizing.

The memory clings like smoke the moment the Shadow King's curse takes him. It haunts me. Every night I wake up in cold sweats. Every time I close my eyes, I see the surrounding people ripped to shreds, the monsters that ransacked my home, it never stops replaying against my closed eyes.

What does this attack bring to the Shadowlands? Soon my father will be gone. I will be king, leading my people into a war I fear we might not win. My people's anger grows each day as they rebuild what the shadows destroyed.

I close my eyes, trying to draw strength from the steady heat of the sun.

Our ancestors came here centuries ago, settling in a land stripped of magic. We survive without it, thrive without it, until the shadows rise. Then, light answers. My power grows every day. I feel it buzzing just under my skin.

Magic.

But in Luminaria, all magic is outlawed by my father, he hates anything related to magic. I never understood why but his reasoning started to make sense after the shadows attacked. The Watchers make sure of it. They rip out every spark, drag the guilty from their homes, and execute them in the name of protection. Yet light burns within me. It has awakened with the shadows, and it grows stronger each day.

The tips of my fingers glimmer, betraying me. I flex my hand and force it back, burying it beneath my skin.

Kain sees anyway. He always does.

"The world is changing," I murmur. "I feel it in the soil, in the wind. The light is ... alive again."

Fear shadows his features. He knows what it will mean if anyone else discovers this truth. Even for me, a prince, the penalty will be death.

The wind rises suddenly, sharp against my face. A sound echoes within it, vast and beating.

My head snaps up.

There, cutting across the valley, wings. Vast, silver-tipped, glinting in the light. A dragon.

I surge to my feet, heart pounding. "Kain," I whisper, disbelief strangling my voice.

His eyes are wide. "Times are changing," he breathes. "I feel it too."

Dragons were banished from our lands generations ago. The decree is etched in stone: no magical creatures in Luminaria. Yet here one soars, a shadow against the sun.

The air itself hums. Sparks race along my skin, a current that seems to rise from the very earth. Change is coming, undeniable.

I think of my father—the man who has carried the weight of this kingdom with unflinching strength. I long for his counsel, for words to anchor me now. But he is slipping from me. The crown looms nearer with every ragged breath he takes, and the future unravels into threads I cannot yet hold together.

Kain's voice pulls me back. "Do we report it?"

I stare at the dragon until it vanishes into the horizon. My heart aches with fear and with something else. Something that feels like hope or perhaps doom.

The light stirs in my veins, humming, restless. And beyond it, something calls to me. A pull, deep and insistent, tugging at my very soul. We can't report the sighting, because I am humming with magic and they will know. The king of mortals is alive with light magic that should not exist in my land.

The dragon is no coincidence.

It is a sign.

THIRTEEN
SKIA

The rooftop stone is hot beneath my palms, rough and jagged as I cling to its edge. Days pass as I wait for an opportunity, using my magic to take me in and out of the Light Lands and hide on the border of the mountains. My shadows curl around me like a cloak, their whispers slithering into my ears, steadying the hollow ache in my chest. *Too loud, too exposed*, they hiss. One wrong move, and I'll fall. Or be seen. Or both.

I don't care.

From here, I can see him.

The heir of Luminaria.

Meir moves across the sunlit courtyard below, his tunic is loose around him, it is a dark tan and blends in with the desert that surrounds him. His head is covered in a headcloth that leaves only his eyes peeking out. His body is protected by leather armor that covers his chest and arms. His movements are effortless as he spars with another man. He moves effortlessly. His laughter carries across the heat-soaked air, warm and careless.

"Kain, can you keep up?"

His sparring partner, a broad-shouldered man with dark hair pulled back from his face, grunts, lunging toward the prince. Wood clashes, shaking the surrounding air. Dust rises in a shimmering halo around them. In the next heartbeat, Meir twists, fast as lightning, and sends Kain crashing to the ground with his knee pressed against his throat.

I shift, leaning closer. The ledge bites into my stomach. The heat presses against my skin, a suffocating blanket compared to the cool, damp shadows of home. My tongue sticks to the roof of my mouth, and no matter how much water I drink the thirst never leaves me. My sweat seems to disappear from my forehead, evaporating in the air. I can taste the dry tang of stone and ash. Even the air here feels foreign, charged, humming with something I cannot name. It feels like our magic but different, lighter, almost as if the heaviness of the shadows disappears.

A Watcher, the guards of the Light Land, passes below the rooftop, his steps precise, his eyes sharp and searching. The bronze insignia of the sun blazes across his chest plate, and his hand hovers near his weapon. He is hunting shadows; they are always hunting. My shadows still, pressing flat to my skin, holding their breath with me. I hold in my magic, trying to blend in with the roof.

If they see me, if they realize what I am, they won't hesitate. They will end me.

His gaze snaps upward towards me.

I press back, heart hammering, trying to hide my body. I lift my eyes just over the edge, trying to gauge if he sees me. As I lift my hand grabbing ahold of the ledge I feel the corner of the building crumble. The edge of the building falling beneath my hands.

Blue. Burning.

For a heartbeat, the world freezes. His eyes lock on mine, so vivid they burn through the heat haze, cutting straight to my marrow. Something inside me gives way. A tether snapped taut, invisible but undeniable, pulling, pulling straight through my chest.

It is like a string stretched between us.

My breath hitches. My knees buckle. My soul lurches toward his.

Fated.

The word sears through me, not spoken, not whispered, but written into the very marrow of my bones. My shadows shriek in my head, a cacophony of voices. Some furious, some elated, some whispering things I do not understand. Screaming for me to go toward him, to be next to him. My body is consumed by him, his physicality, his stare, his spirit.

I stumble back, the rooftop tilting beneath me. The stone bites my palms as I slip. The Watcher's head whips toward the sound.

Too late.

The ledge crumbles completely. I fall.

The wind tears at me, and for one terrible instant I think this is it. My death, broken bones on sunlit stone. But then my shadows roar and take over without my command. They surge from me in a torrent, a living tide of black that catches my body midair. They flip me, cradle me, slow my fall until I hit the stones hard but alive.

Gasps ring out. A guard shouts.

"Shadow wielder!"

The word is a curse, a weapon, a death sentence.

I bolt.

Let's get out of here, I command my shadows, and their powers wrap around me as I run.

Arrows hiss through the air, slicing past my ear, so close I feel the fletching brush my skin. I feel the sting and blood dripping from my ear.. Another sparks against the wall at my back, showering me in dust and stone chips. Boots pound across the courtyard as voices rise, alarm bells echoing like war drums.

My shadows lash outward, striking the air. One arrow dissolves into ash before it pierces me; another bends mid-flight as if the air itself curves to shield me. They hiss in triumph, begging me to let them *feed*.

"No," I gasp, lungs burning. "Not here!"

I tear through the alleys, narrow streets twisting between pale stone walls. The scent of spices and smoke clings to the air, undercut with sweat and iron. My boots scrape across cobblestones as I dart past abandoned stalls. The bright silks of the market flutter in my wake. Shouts follow me, closer, closer, always closer. The heat is exhausting as I run against the sand roads.

I risk one glance over my shoulder.

And see him.

Meir.

He didn't join the chase. He just stands there in the courtyard, blue eyes burning into mine. The surrounding light seems to flare brighter, the edges of his form almost too radiant to look at. He doesn't move. He didn't need to. The tether is there, thrumming between us with every frantic beat of my heart.

My chest clenches, a tight knot of anxiety. Panic clawing at me.

I need to get away.

Faster.

My shadows surge harder, dragging me faster, faster, wrapping my legs in strength not my own.

I can't breathe.

I can't think.

I ran from him.

 From that bond.

The alleys blur. The bells toll louder. Guards shouting. My shadows keen in my ears, shrill and exultant, whispering things I didn't want to hear: *Mate. Destiny. Light. Yours. Ours.*

"Shut up," I hiss, my voice breaking.

But the bond thrums, like a second heartbeat, like a brand pressing into my chest, burning.

I stumble into a narrow passage, press myself against the wall, chest heaving. The world tilts. My mind overflows in thoughts and spins making me dizzy. My shadows wrap tight, their touch cold against my fever-hot skin.

I found him.

The one the Seer spoke of. The light. The prince. My soul's tether.

And I flee.

Because if I stay—if I let the bond pull me closer—I will never escape it.

And when my father finds out...

The whispers of my shadows curl around me, dark and inevitable.

You cannot run from fate, Skia. Not forever.

But I will try. Gods, I will try.

I run until my legs give out, until the bond's thrumming dulls to a distant ache, and I allow my shadows to transport me. I ran.

I ran from my soulmate.

FOURTEEN
SKIA

The world shifts. Stone gives way to grass, heat to damp earth. My knees hit the ground, fingers clawing through blades of green until the panic thudding in my chest slows to something survivable. The valley stretches around me, silent and secret, mist curling along its edges as if it wants to hide me.

A shadow passes overhead.

"Lyra," I breathe.

She descends with a screech that shakes the trees, her silver wings stirring the air into storms. Dust scatters and leaves whip into spirals. Violet eyes lock on me, molten and sharp. Judgment. Disappointment. She lands with a thunderous crack, claws gouging deep furrows into the earth.

Her snout lowers until sulfur-hot breath rolls over me in waves. My shadows twitch uneasily, whispering of submission, but I ignore them. I press my forehead against the cool steel of her scales, closing my eyes.

"Yeah, nice to see you too," I mutter. Her chest rumbles, deep and resonant, not with anger but with something softer. It sounds like a purr, an oversized, dangerous cat who both scalds and forgives me in the same breath. She lets no harm come to me. My ultimate protector.

When the valley quiets, I lay in the cool grass playing with my shadows, weaving them in and out. My shadows stir at the motion, rising, shaping themselves into forms. I force them into butterflies—black wings edged in silver, fragile things that flutter and spiral in the night air. Beautiful. Deadly. A lie dressed as grace.

Even their elegance can't smother the truth.

I had felt it. It is undeniable.

The bond.

Fated mates.

The words hiss, a venomous whisper, a sound like a snake's strike against the dim backdrop of my mind. I remember the stories, their ink a dark stain on the aged parchment in the castle library. The many times that

Raven and I had snuck into the library searching for answers. Moonlight, cool and blue, fractured through stained glass, painting patterns on the pages. The air was thick with the scent of old paper and dust, the hushed atmosphere heavy with tales of old conflicts and shadowed magic. Whispers of devotion, like the soft rustle of silk, of souls bound before the gods, of a love that a cold blade cannot sever or a shadow extinguish. Fairy tales, I thought. Fantasies.

And now the string is tied to me.

To him.

The heir of Luminaria.

My chest tightens. My parents were never like that. Silence is where my mother fled. I never knew her. My father's cruelty is the only constant I know. I accept solitude as my inheritance. Darkness is my companion. Yet fate binds me to the one person I should never touch. The one thing I cannot have. Mortal from the Light Lands.

I press my palms to the earth. It thrums beneath me like a heartbeat, answering mine. The land feels alive, pulsing with each breath I take. Storm clouds mass together at the mountains' edge, thunder rolling low. Shadows stir, restless, tasting my fear.

And somewhere beyond those peaks, I can feel my father's darkness hunting. He is coming for me. I can only hide for so long before his claws are at my throat.

If he ever discovers what I have found—who I have found—he will raze the Light Lands to ash, salt their soil, drink their screams.

My breath catches. My fists clench, nails biting into my palms. The Seer's words press against my mind, relentless, inescapable.

You are the answer. His power will awaken the gods. Together, you will unite what has been torn apart.

How can that be true when everything inside me screams I am ruin, not salvation?

Fate has tied me to the enemy. To a mortal prince with sky-blue eyes, flooding my soul like the sea. To the one soul I am doomed to destroy.

And still hidden beneath the fear, beneath the despair, my soul whispers its undeniable truth.

I found him.

And no matter how far I run, I know I can never forget him.

FIFTEEN
SEER

The pounding rattles the door, threatening to rip it from its hinges. Each strike reverberates through the floorboards, through my bones. My hand trembles as it finds the cold iron latch.

When the door creaks open, he is already upon me.

Morthal's icy silver eyes blaze, and his hand clamps around my throat. My back slams against the wall, the air crushed from my lungs. "Where is she?" he growls, his spit flecking my cheek.

I claw at his grip, wheezing, but his shadows lend him strength. Pain lances up my neck—yet I smile.

His rage means only one thing.

She is gone.

The girl has left. She has defied him. She has chosen her path. The necklace at my throat beats in triumph, as if it already knew.

My smile ignites his fury. His hand cracks against my cheek, the copper taste of blood filling my mouth. Still, I laugh. My hands burn hot as I summon my flame, searing his skin until he roars and staggers back. Smoke curls from his face, the smell of charred flesh sharp in the air.

"You dare?" he shouts, shadows gathering like wolves at his heels.

"You are mistaken," I rasp, my fire curling into a rope that snaps tight around his throat, sizzling against his skin. I pull him close, so close our eyes meet—my amethyst fire against his endless dark. "I do not answer to you, Morthal. I never have and I never will. You may think you have control over the Seers, but you will never have control over me."

His sneer falters as I hiss the words meant to wound. I see it gnawing at him, the memories of our past flashing behind his eyes. The words leave my mouth with fury pounding behind them.

"The day Skia sees you for what you are is the day you fall, and you should worry because if she left, she's close."

His shadows recoil. For one heartbeat, fear flickers behind his fury. My words, stabbing old wounds, he tries to forget.

I press harder, my petite frame overpowering his strength. "You are nothing without her. The power you flaunt. Stolen. The crown you wear. Borrowed. Without her light chained to your darkness, you are ash."

His rage turns brittle, his grip slackens, he freezes. He knows it is true. He knows that the power that flows within him is not sustainable. His immortality, his strength, all washed away when he stole her power from her all those years ago.

With a snarl, he shoves free of my flame and storms from the cottage, slamming the door so hard the rafters shake. "For this, Seer, you will rot," he snarls. "No vision will save you. No Seer will follow after you. I will erase your entire line from this world."

Silence swallows the room when he is gone. My throat burns, my cheek throbs, but still I stand straight. Still, I smile.

Because the threads of fate shift.

He is right about one thing: my days are numbered. But so are his.

I press a hand to the amulet at my chest. Its green fire pulses with the voices of the Seers before me. Skia's path is dangerous, twisted with shadows and betrayal, but she carries within her the strength to end him. To end this.

I will see her warned. Guided. Protected.

Lucille will be my messenger.

And when the King of Shadows finally falls, it will be at the hands of the girl he tried to break. His ruin has been born from the very weapon he forged.

SIXTEEN
MEIR

The Watcher sprints up behind me, his face tight with panic. "Sir, she vanished. One moment she was there and the next, gone. We need the Hunters. For your protection, Your Majesty, it's not safe with shadows around. They should know that someone from the Shadowlands is here."

His words claw me back to reality, tearing me from the haze she left behind. I stop short, hand raised in dismissal. "No. You are dismissed."

The Watcher hesitates, but I don't look back.

How can I explain what is happening?

The pull I feel toward this woman defies reason. My soul recognizes her as if I have been searching for her throughout lifetimes. Her shadows should frighten me, but somehow, I am drawn to them, compelled to be the light that balances them. She is a stranger, but already her absence carves a hole in my chest. I will find her again. I have to.

"Your Majesty," the Watcher presses, "if you don't act—look at the king's condition. The same fate—"

"You are dismissed." I shout.

The Hunters can never know of me. If they come, they will feel my light burning where no mortal's should. They will sense my power growing. The stirring land will be sensed by them. They will end me before I even take the throne.

The Hunters have no masters. They answer to no king, no crown. Through the years, they spent more time in the Shadowlands. For centuries, they've executed anyone touched by magic that was born in the Light Lands. They are the gods' law made flesh, born of the age when divine hands shaped mountains and rivers. When the gods withdrew, they left the Hunters behind to enforce their decrees. Now they linger at the edges of both kingdoms, their judgment absolute. To summon them would be to invite my execution.

Kain catches up with me as I cross the glass threshold of the castle. Sunlight spills through the walls, every movement visible to those outside. Our lives have always been a spectacle, but now, with light sparking at my fingertips, the transparency feels dangerous. At any moment, someone could see what I am becoming.

"Kain," I murmur, "we're not safe here. I'm not safe here. The king's fate is sealed, and once he's gone, the shadows will move against us. We can't stay."

He freezes, eyes searching mine. I can see the weight of what I am asking him to shoulder. The risk of exile, of treason. But I also see the answer in his gaze. Kain has never abandoned me.

"We'll go," I say softly, as much to myself as to him. "We'll keep appearances, get through the ball and whatever else. But after that, we ride for answers, we go into the Dark Forest."

Silence stretches. Then Kain's hand clasps my shoulder, his grip steady, his smile faint but fierce. "Then let's not waste time. Whatever awaits, we face it together."

Relief loosens the knot in my chest. "We'll need supplies. Horses. A plan to disappear."

He smirks. "I'll handle it, brother. You just keep breathing."

I laugh once, short and brittle, before the weight returns. Why now? Why did the light awaken in me only as the world shifted beneath our feet?

The throne room swallows me as I enter; its brilliance refracts across crystal walls. To the people who bow as I pass, I must look every bit the heir. But I feel like a fraud. A man with outlawed power coursing through his veins, a secret that can burn everything down.

My thoughts turn to her. The girl is cloaked in shadows. Her green eyes meet mine only for a breath, but in that breath something inside me breaks open. A bond, undeniable and raw. I don't know what it means, but her green eyes haunt the back of my eyelids anytime they close. She is a ghost in my mind haunting every thought.

I clench my jaw, forcing myself into the rhythm of duty. The coronation ball will proceed as planned, what should be filled with excitement, leaves my grief on display. The coronation will come, a momentous occasion eagerly awaited by all, except me. Politics, alliances, whispers of war, all of it demands my focus. But behind every mask I wear, I will be searching.

For her.

For the shadow that has become my light.

SEVENTEEN
SEER

21 years ago

My body courses with pain as the contraction takes over, and I push. The baby's cry splits the still air, shrill and insistent, cutting through the sterile quiet of the birthing room. My body shakes as the midwife takes her and places her in my arms. I hold her slick, blood-streaked body close. She is so small, and I am in awe of this tiny human in my arms. Her warmth presses against my chest as my body convulses, pushing out the afterbirth, a crimson offering to the gods who have marked this moment long before it came to pass.

She is not mine in the way most babies are claimed. She is the Shadow Goddess's gift, placed in my womb as a vessel. I carry her not only in body but in vision. Even before this night, she has plagued me with glimpses of what she will become, strength wrapped in shadows, a blade tempered by suffering, a light buried deep within darkness.

The midwife trembles at my side, her hands shaking as she swaddles the child. Though she had witnessed dozens of births, she flinches as the surrounding air crackles with unseen energy, the very walls alive with a hum that resonates through my bones. The scent of blood, sweat, and iron fills the chamber, undercut by something stranger — the metallic tang of magic, raw and ancient.

The infant's hair, damp and black as midnight, clings to her head. Her eyes flutter open, revealing a flash of green so piercing it steals my breath. They are the same color as the emerald that pulses at my throat — the amulet of the Seers, heavy with the souls and visions of those who came before me. In her gaze, I see not just a child, but the echo of awakening futures.

Tears slip unbidden down my cheeks, falling onto her small face. She does not cry again. Instead, she stares up at me, calm, almost knowing and the weight of prophecy settles heavier upon me than the babe herself.

The Shadow Goddess, Niaxias, entrusts me with more than life. She places into my arms a weapon, not to be wielded by me, but to one day undo the very tyrant who thinks to rule unchecked. This child is the hinge on which the fate of two worlds rests.

I press her to my breast, and as she nurses, I feel it. Power siphoning through me into her, her tiny body drinking not only milk but strength. My limbs weaken as she grows, as if the very act of sustaining her transfers pieces of my essence into hers.

And then comes the vision.

Shadows gather at the edges of the room, whispering, pulling the air cold around me. My skin erupts in goosebumps, my breath stutters in my throat, and sweat trickles down my temple. I see her future as a tapestry. Threads of ruin and rebirth, of fire consuming and light returning. Faces blur before me, some joyous, some broken, all bound to her path. I see her wielding her gift as both salvation and destruction.

When the vision releases me, I collapse against the stone wall, trembling, the child still latched and drinking. My heart pounds with the truth I can no longer deny.

This is no ordinary girl. She is the one who would end the Shadow King. She is the one who would tear apart the world and stitch it together anew.

And I am the only one who knows.

EIGHTEEN
MEIR

The castle buzzes with restless energy, preparations for the ball humming like a hive around me. One day remains before lords and ladies will pour through the gates, unwelcome mouths asking questions, unwelcome eyes prying into cracks I can no longer conceal. And through it all, my father lies upstairs, clinging to life with shallow breaths.

The glass hallway blazes with sunlight, every step a reminder that there is no hiding here. A castle of crystal leaves no shadows to vanish into, no corner for privacy. My patience thins with every nod, every bow, every forced conversation. I need answers, not silks or banquets. Where does my light come from? What was my mother hiding? Did the light live within her as well?

Memories come in fragments. Blonde hair. Laughter like bells. Arms that hold me and make the world feel safe.

Then nothing. A question where her leaving should have been. I remember her, for all the happiness she gave me. My father did not speak of her. I carry her only in flashes, and in this light that burns in me like a piece of her soul left behind.

My chest tightens. My pulse throbs against my temples; heat rises in my neck. I clench my fists until nails dig crescents into my palms, fighting the weight of memory and of expectation. The ballroom's clamor — silks rustling, voices chattering, laughter carrying — presses in like a tide, threatening to drown me. And beneath it all, the question looms. What happens when they see what I am?

Light flares from my fingertips at the worst of times, uncontrolled, wild. What will my people do when they realize their prince, soon their king, carries a magic long outlawed? Will they crown me or hunt me?

"Meir?"

I blink back to the present. Kain stands at my shoulder, brows drawn together. I miss his words.

"I—sorry. What?"

"There are more responses to the ball," he repeats patiently. "The lords and ladies will be here. They expect a smooth transition."

I nod, hearing his words but not feeling them. My mind runs ahead, a tangle of contingencies and fears. The ball is no celebration; it is a stage. And if my power reveals itself under the eyes of the Hunters, under the weight of those who already doubt me, it is the end.

I excuse myself and leave the crowded hall, climbing the stairs toward my father's chambers. Light fractures through every pane of glass around me, throwing prisms across my path. I long for shade, for a veil against the relentless brightness. The light is inescapable, around me, within me.

His chamber is quiet but for the rasp of his breath. Shadows marble his skin, black veins spiderweb across his body, leaving only the hood of his eyes untouched. He is frail, barely a man, the shell of the king I once knew. Each breath seems to consume all he has left.

I sink into the chair beside him, folding my head into my hands. The silence crushes me. The weight of a kingdom and needing my father to help guide me. I feel alone. Alone endlessly.

When I finally lift my gaze, I take his hand. It is so icy and thin, even under the weight of blankets. A plea tightens in my chest. *Stay. Teach me what I do not yet know. Don't leave me on this throne unprepared.*

But his gaze is glazed over and distant, unfocused. The man, who had once been unshakable, now teeters on the edge of the void.

I stay until the rhythm of his breathing changes, uneven, faltering. Something is not right; the look of his body barely holding on. I rise, reaching for the door, yelling for a healer. And then came one last rattling breath, a sound that stills the world.

I freeze, my hand on the latch.

The silence that follows is absolute.

The king is dead.

My knees buckle. The floor meets me hard, and the room swims, blurring at the edges. My chest heaves as if the air itself has thickened. My heart pounds like a war drum, hollow in my ears. I hear the footsteps stepping around me, the commotion as people pour in, and I have no recognition, no ability to stand or do anything else.

    My father is dead.

    And the throne, cursed and waiting, now belongs to me.

NINETEEN
SKIA

The city rings with the tolling of death knells. Bells echo through the cobbled streets, each strike reverberating with grief and duty. Yellow roses litter the roads, petals crushing beneath the feet of mourners. Banners of Luminaria's crest droop from balconies, limp and heavy in the stagnant air.

The Light King is dead.

The ball is put on hold as the kingdom prepares for the funeral for the King. Every day the bells ring, and the city is in mourning.

And his son, Meir, will ascend. The one with eyes that already unsettles my soul. My fated mate. The prophecy's choice.

I hide in the shadows. I see the people lining the streets, not for the ball but for a funeral. Mourning replaces the laughter and music, which cease to exist.

Hidden in the shadows on the building's edge, I survey the city below. I watch as the mourners, faces etched with grief, slowly fill the city square. The nobles dress in white and gold silks, and commoners hold yellow roses in their hands. Clutching at this last part of the king and all that he stood for.

In the square, the air is thick with heat and the smell of incense, and the king's body lay in the center. His body rests on a pyre awaiting to be turned to ash. The king, a stark figure against the dark wood, an empty husk awaiting its fiery transformation. I can see the resemblance between Meir and his father, or what once was. My stomach knots with sadness.

Scanning the square, I see just at the center of the square by the pyre, Meir. His golden hair is unkempt; shadows carve unrest under his eyes. When he looks up, I do not see a king or the Prince of Light. I see a son, a boy who is hollow with the loss of his father. I can see his lips moving softly, words only meant for the man that could no longer answer.

An ache claws within, twisting and breaking. Shadows around me shift, restless. Emptiness. His emptiness.

Whispers intensify the ache, a sharp, piercing sensation. The bond tugs, a desperate pull to comfort him. His pain floods me, a crushing weight. A sob escapes and a single tear traces a path down my cheek.

The High Priestess raises her voice and calls upon the God of Light. The crowd echoes her prayer, a wave of grief that rises like a wave ready to crash. Meir clenches his jaw, his shoulders sag, and I see it then, his struggle with the weight of it all. The kingdom, the crown, the grief he could not show.

And yet, I see it. I feel it.

The High Priestess brings a torch to Meir, and he takes it in his hands. I can see them shaking. He rises and lowers the torch to the pyre. The fire began to consume his father. I see him standing there, his eyes reflecting the flickering light of the flame as it consumes someone precious to him.

The people leave, and my shadows whisper. *We cannot stay here any longer.* Yet I cannot move; my gaze locks on him. The flickering flames cast dancing shadows that seem to lick at his grief-etched face. Higher they dance, the heat a tangible wave. I long to run, to mend him, the sight of his pain cracks me open.

But I can't move forward, I can't answer the call, I bury it instead and call on my shadows and disappear.

TWENTY
SKIA

Days have passed since the King's funeral. I dress in silence, tugging at lace with trembling fingers. My hair falls in waves over my shoulders, too soft, too open. The large tent around me echoes with the weeks I have spent here, waiting. I look down at the darkness that is covering my body, the black lace layering over my skin.

The shadows whisper, *not enough.*

They are right. In the light kingdom, color is life. Even at the King's funeral, amidst the somber atmosphere, the vibrant colors seemed to glow and shimmer.

Darkness will betray me. I exhale and summon a spark of shadow to lick across my gown. Black turns to fiery scarlet and vibrant orange, the fire's dance mirroring in my face. My pale skin flushed, a warmth I'd never known, as if I stand in the sun. For the first time, I see a stranger.

Coming from the tent, Lyra huffs as if unimpressed. I give her one last scratch beneath the chin before I step into the valley and call the shadows to take me. In an instant, I emerge in a Luminaria alley, the hem of my dress brushing cobblestones.

The ballroom swallows me whole. Music soars, violins echoing off the crystal walls, while gowns flash with color and gold under chandeliers. The air is thick with perfume and the buzz of whispered alliances. I press against a marble pillar, grounding myself against the stone.

Then a hand brushes mine.

I flinch and turn.

Meir.

Close enough to feel his warmth against my skin, his breath against my ear. "Strange," he murmurs, voice low, "I feel like I've seen you before, perhaps wrapped in shadows."

I can't meet his eyes. My throat pounds as the anxiety thrums through my body. Not until his fingers brush my hair behind my shoulder. Then I look up.

And the world stills.

The pull inside me is instant, violent. *Mate*. His blue eyes burn into mine, ocean-deep, storm-tossed. "Dance with me," he whispers. I feel my breath catch as he gently, but firmly, pulls me into the dance.

The ballroom blurs around us. I'm lost in his grip, my heart pounding and thoughts racing. He interrupts my thoughts, "I don't understand it, but there is something about you, my soul craves you and my dreams are haunted by you. The air changes when I'm near you."

The crowd vanishes. Only his hand at my back, firm and certain, guiding me across polished glass floors. Only his gaze, unwavering, asks questions he cannot speak aloud. For the first time, the shadows within me hush.

"You must be mistaken," I whisper, but I feel it, the pull, the need to be with him.

Silence replaces the echoes of the shadows in my head. Silence. A tear slips free. He catches it with his thumb, then, gods help me, brushes it against his lips, tasting it. As though he could carry my sorrow with him.

"People are watching," I remind him as we glide across the dance floor.

"Let them," he purrs into my ear, his breath tickling, "I will trade every crown, every oath, just to keep you here in my arms tonight."

The world tilts. My chest burns. The racing thoughts break the dam that had been holding them back. I break from his arms and run, slipping through the crowd, past the music, out into the courtyard. His voice follows, sharp, desperate.

"I didn't get your name."

I flee.

I feel the power grow as I step one foot in front of the other. Their darkness engulfs me; I cannot control it. My breath is racing, and I feel like everything is too much, too tight, suffocating. I can't gain control; too many words fly through my head, and I can't grasp anything. The world is gone, and I see darkness spinning around me. Like a vortex, it snuffs out any control I have.

They surge, wild and ravenous, erupting from my skin in a storm I cannot contain. My body twists in their grip, every breath a gasp. Too much. Too tight. Suffocating. I stumble, choking, the ground rushing up — and then light.

Blinding, searing, splitting through the storm.

Hands catch me before I fall.

Blue eyes.

Meir.

TWENTY-ONE
MEIR

I chase after her as she flees the ballroom because the moment, I see her green eyes, the world shifts.

The pull is immediate. As if my soul was waiting for her all along.

Her shadows swallow her. The same shadows that devoured my father and made me king now curling tight around her body, twisting, choking, pulling her under. Any sane man would have run. Instead, I step closer.

Light flares from my hands, instinctive, uncontrollable. It rips through her storm, pressing back the darkness until I reach her. I catch her arms. Her skin is icy, my warmth pouring into her like fire. Her clouded eyes clear, green finding me in the chaos, and in that instant — I am home.

Her fear stabs me like a blade. My hand rises, clumsy, to her cheek, tracing the line of her face as if I can memorize it. My thumb brushes her lips, and she draws a sharp breath. Then she pulls away, shadows curling around her once more. And just like that, she vanishes.

Gone.

I stand in the empty street, breathless, my hands outstretched to nothing. It feels like half my soul has been torn away. The crown could burn, the kingdom could fall — none of it mattered. I would find her again.

A hand grips my shoulder. Kain. "You ran off. The whole ball is waiting for you," he smirks, then falters when he sees my face.

"The shadows," I rasp. "They took my father. They belong to her."

"And now they've taken a piece of you," he finishes softly. He knows. He always knew.

I force myself to breathe, to stand straighter, though my chest still aches with the loss of her. "She's the one from the alley," I admit. "I'll find her again. She has the answers we need — about the shadows, about why the land is changing, maybe about me. I'll find her."

Kain studies me for a long moment, then nods. "Then tomorrow, we leave."

The masquerade of duty would continue through the night, but my decision is made. The hunt begins.

TWENTY-TWO
SKIA

The shadows curl around me as I walk down the cobblestone street of the Darklands, the gas lamps flickering overhead, casting long, distorted shapes that dance with the rain. My lacy black dress, clinging to my skin, drags along the wet pavement, its delicate fabric already stained and soiled. The rain is a relentless torrent, pouring down in sheets, washing away the city's grime and mirroring the turmoil within me. I am invisible, lost in the deluge, a ghost drifting through the heart of the city. My shadows brought me here, a place I am no longer welcomed. My tears, hot and bitter, mingle with the cold, relentless raindrops dripping down my face, indistinguishable from the storm's embrace. Each footstep echoes hollowly, the only sound besides the drumming of the rain and the distant rumble of thunder, as I continue my solitary journey. A damp chill seeps into my bones, reflecting the coldness that settles in my heart. The city, once a vibrant tapestry of life and laughter, is now a bleak and echoing prison, and I, its silent, unseen inhabitant.

He is coming for you, the shadows whisper. Goosebumps spread across my body. A shadow passes overhead, followed by the roaring of my dragon. I do not know why my shadows brought me here. The fear of my father finding me after everything I've done rips my stomach apart.

"Why," I curse aloud to my shadows. *Why bring me here?*

I feel anxiety creeping up my body, the tears breaking the dam that I held back for so long. I want to collapse, I want to give up.

A twig snaps jolting my attention from my internal spiral, sending my shadows on full alert.

A figure steps from the tree line. Tall. Gaunt. His eyes, chips of ice. He raises his hand, and a spear of pure shadow forms. It streaks toward me, aimed at my heart. My shadows engulf me, the world shifts, and I'm closer to the forest. The shadow lances the air where I'd been standing. Lyra roars, her fire splitting the night, but the man only laughs, a hollow sound, before vanishing into the trees. Her shadow passes over, her wings spinning dirt in the air.

I force my body to move, muscles screaming in protest, summoning what strength remains. Every breath is ragged, tasting of smoke and rain, but survival urges me on. I summon my shadows, and in a flash, the suffocating city disappears. When my vision clears, I'm back in the sun-drenched valley. Dirt whips in the wind, the dry heat overwhelming, clinging to me as if to remind me of gentler things. Lyra follows emerging from shadows, wings cracking like thunder as she lands behind me. For a moment, I let the sunlight soak into me, trying to banish the chill of the shadows.

But even here, safety feels fragile. Guilt crushes me—bringing Lyra into danger, failing to stay hidden, failing to control myself. And under it all, the memory of *him* lingers. The warmth of his hands, the piercing blue of his eyes, the tether I cannot sever no matter how I try.

The tears flow, there is no stopping them, my mind feels like claws are twisting and ripping. My body shakes and each heave between my sobs I fight to bring air to my chest.

I turn to Lyra, pressing my forehead against her scaled snout. "You can't stay. Not here. You need to go back to the Shadowlands. Somewhere safe, beyond the Shadowlands, if you must." My voice cracks as the command leaves my lips.

Lyra huffs, smoke curling from her nostrils. She boops her large snout at me, bringing my attention to her face. I can see the pain etched behind her purple eyes.

I push the words out, anyway. "I'll be okay here. I need to find Meir. He's the answer I've been searching for, the prophecy– his power—his light—it's stronger than anything I've ever felt. Maybe stronger than my father's shadows."

My mind races with a thousand thoughts I can't get out and I feel lost. Nothing I saw makes sense but I know I need her to leave, to get away from the danger that haunts me. A friend I need to protect.

Friend.

Raven should be here. She always has been. My anchor in the chaos, reckless but loyal, reckless but *mine.* Yet when the shadows whisper her name, they do not sound mournful. They hiss, venomous and sharp: *She chooses her own path now. She does not run beside you.*

A cold ache pierces my chest. Loyalty, I remind myself. Raven has always been loyal. But even as I cling to the memory of her laughter, her sharp wit, the way she could pull me from the depths—I can't shake the suspicion that her absence is not by chance. What if she has chosen? What if the darkness in her heart bends differently than mine, sharper, hungrier?

I shove the thought away, but it lingers like a knife against my ribs.

Lyra huffs, and obeys, her massive wings lifting her into the sky. The emptiness she leaves behind is suffocating.

I shoulder my pack and call on my shadows again. In the blink of an eye, the valley vanishes, and I'm standing in a narrow alley beside Luminaria's castle. My shadows coil around me like a cloak as I strip off my gown. I pull on black trousers, a fitted black top, and heavy leather boots. The moment I lace the last one, I stumble on a rock heading for the sandy street.

Before I can catch myself, a hand reaches out—strong, steady—and hauls me to my feet. I don't need to look to know. I *feel* him. That magnetic pull.

Meir.

His blue eyes lock on mine, intense and searching, and the world narrows to just that look. Behind him, his companion waits with packs strapped to his shoulders. They're leaving. Disappearing from the kingdom.

"Going somewhere?" I ask, my voice sharper than I intend. I'm on edge.

He arches a brow. "Yes," he answers, suspicion in his tone. "What is your name? You left in such a rush from the ball…"

I tilt my head, fighting to keep my shadows from stirring. "Wouldn't you like to know? Maybe you aren't worthy of my name, King." I snap back, the irritation building with each minute passing.

A smile curls his lips, maddeningly sure. He reaches for the strap of my pack, pulling me closer. "It looks like you're going somewhere too. Perhaps our paths are meant to cross." His voice drops lower, teasing. "I think you'll find my company useful. So… what do you say?

Join us?" His lips linger near my ear and my heart pounds giving away my illusion of calm.

I pull back and cross my arms, pretending his nearness doesn't ignite every nerve in my body. "Fine. But only if you have a horse to spare."

He laughs, the sound low and warm. "Demanding little shadow," he comes close again. Like a lever pulling him back.

"Oh, full of light and smart remarks aren't you, your majesty?" I can see it, a trace of fear, as I acknowledge his power. His illegal power for the Light Lands.

"Okay, little shadow, you can ride with me." He winks at me.

He winks.

Infuriating.

And though I sigh in feigned reluctance, my heart betrays me—racing, aching, desperate. Even as the shadows whisper betrayal in my ear, I step closer to him.

TWENTY-THREE
SKIA

The leather straps creak as I fasten my bag to the saddle of the black stallion, grounding myself in the rhythm of preparation. The horse snorts, impatiently. The sun blares, making sweat bead on my hairline.

When I look back, Meir is already watching me, arms crossed, that same arrogant smirk tugging at his lips as though he's already won a game I didn't agree to play. His white cotton shirt hangs loose, he did not wear his usual royal uniform. His honey colored beard almost blends in with the golden bandanna that hangs at his neck.

"So, what's your name, little shadow?" His voice is deep, smooth, and laced with amusement.

I roll my eyes before I can stop myself. "Ski, Your Highness," I mock, letting the title drip with sarcasm. His smirk widens, infuriatingly pleased with himself. He walks toward me, and climbs onto the back of the horse, effortlessly.

"Do they even have horses in the Shadowlands?" he asks, slouching lazily in the saddle, his arm drapes over the pommel. His eyes, blue, blazing in the sunlight, catch mine, and for a fleeting moment, I can't look away, sucked into the trance of his eyes. I blink, realizing he had asked a question, and I was staring for too long.

"Dragons mostly," I say, looking at the horse that stood before me. It stands almost past my head, its shining black coat seeming to glitter in the light. It sighs as I take it in, almost as if it is letting me know I'm safe.

Focus, if I can ride a dragon, I can manage a horse.

"Do you need my help, little shadow?" Meir is assessing me.

"No," I snap.

My shadows stir restlessly, feeding on my doubt. I bite them back and, without waiting for permission, swing onto the horse, settling in front of him.

His warmth presses against my back. His arms slide around me, reaching for the reins, and the brush of his fingers across my waist sends an unwanted thrill sparking through me. The bond tugs at my soul like a chain I can't break, a cruel joke fate is playing. He is my enemy. My mate. The enemy. And he does not even know.

As we move farther from the city, the ground shifts. Dry dirt replaces sand, crunching underfoot. The air cools, carrying the faint scent of grass and moss. Ahead, the Geheimnis Forest looms, its canopy of towering trees swallowing the path in shadow. The silence thickens as we enter, pressing down like a weight. No wind. No birdsong. Only the faint electric hum of magic thrumming through the air.

"So," Meir says at last, his tone deceptively casual. "Did you come to Luminaria to admire the chaos? Or just to see if your shadows were successful in killing the king?"

His words cut through me like an arrow. My heart drops, heavy and cold. He suspects me.

Taking a steadying breath, I force my voice even. "Your Highness, my shadows were not the ones that killed your king."

His body tightens behind me. "I have my reasons," he breathes against my ear.

"Then say them," I snap, rage bubbling over. "Or are your accusations as empty as the throne you defend?"

His voice, deep and dangerous, brushes against my ear, "You think me blind?"

"The only thing my shadows have destroyed is me." I say, my chest heaving, the confession making me feel light.

"I see more than you might think," he murmurs, his voice softer.

"Then see me for what I am, not for what they tell you to believe." The words whisper from my mouth as I turn to look into his ocean eyes. They are soft, and his breath is uneven.

The forest thickens around us. Towering green leaves block the light, turning the path into a shifting patchwork of shadow. The air presses close, heavy and watchful, as though unseen creatures prowl just beyond sight. The horse trembles beneath us, reacting to the forest's pulse. The silence consumes the words before we speak them.

As we travel further into the forest, the light grows dimmer, the sun darkens. What little light pierces the canopy almost vanishes. I feel Meir's body becoming more alert.

After riding for most of the day, Kain breaks the silence. "It would be wise to camp. Pushing through on horseback after dark will bring us the attention we don't want."

The temperature plummets as we dismount. Goosebumps ripple over my arms where Meir's warmth had been. He unpacks the supplies from the horses, moving with an ease born of practice, while Kain busies himself building the fire.

Compared to Meir, Kain is taller. His onyx hair is close-cropped and dark, and his skin is tanner than Meir's. His eyes, burnt orange almost golden, unsettlingly familiar, catch the firelight and seem almost to glow. Mortals are not meant to look like that, but the people of Luminaria carry strangeness in their blood.

The fire crackles, spitting embers into the darkening air. Meir worked with efficiency, Kain with quiet precision. I wrap my arms around myself, fighting off the creeping chill, my gaze drawn again and again to the shifting shadows of the forest.

Every rustle might be a threat.

I stand and cross my arms, looking at both of them. "What are the sleeping arrangements?" I ask, my voice is sharper than I intend, frustration at the lack of planning. I had no bedroll to sleep in just a small bag with food, coins, and my cloak.

Kain looks up, a grin curling on his lips. "Princess, you won't be sharing a blanket with me." He glances at Meir, his smirk widening. "What about you, Your Highness? Want to keep her warm?" Meir drops a log at his feet.

I stand, snatching the log he'd dropped and throwing it into the fire. Embers spray upward, hissing against the silence of the forest. The embers twirling together a mix of light and darkness playing together.

TWENTY-FOUR
MEIR

Her eyes, the color of polished emeralds, track our every movement with unnerving intensity. She observes each subtle shift. The break of a branch beneath our boots, the rustle of a water flask. Soon, our small fire, a flickering beacon in the encroaching darkness of the forest, will vanish, and the air will grow colder, a harbinger of the long, frigid night that stretches before us.

I lower the packs onto the damp earth, the heavy canvas thudding softly, and arrange them for sleeping, makeshift barriers against the chill. We cannot risk keeping the fire lit; the flames and the scent of smoke will only attract unwanted company. And yet, deep down, I know no precaution will matter. Whatever stalks these woods will find us whether we hide or not.

"Ski," I try, breaking the silence. "Is your name short for anything?"

She raises an eyebrow, arms crossing, her silence sharp as a blade.

Kain lifts his eyebrow to me, leaning back against the tree and crossing his arms, a smirk growing on his face as he observes me.

"No?" I push. "Would you rather we speak of the shadows... the ones from your land that killed my father?"

The words slip out before I can stop them. Her face flickers with pain, awareness, and something else, but she offers nothing. I turn away, searching through our supplies, though the sting of my own question lingers.

"Bringing this up again?" She asks, her body once again tense.

"No, my little shadow, I just enjoy watching you squirm." I say my words smoothly, almost giving away the ache that pounds in my chest, wanting to be near her. Consumed by her.

Did she know the danger of my powers? I carry the power to burn the shadows into nothing. Does she understand how close I stand on the edge of control?

She is someone I cannot trust. And yet... something inside me longs for her still. Like I have known her in a thousand lives before this one, her presence is both a warning and a homecoming.

I force a smirk. "Well, little shadow, you're lucky enough to bunk with me. Take it as my security—to ensure you're not dragged off in the middle of the night."

"Great," she spits, rolling her eyes. She curls into the pack with theatrical defiance, claiming as much space as possible.

I cannot help the smile tugging at my lips. "At least you'll stay warm."

When I slip in behind her, her body is icy against my warmth. She shivers, until I place my hand over her stomach, steadying her. Slowly, the tremors fade, her breathing even, and she melts into my arms. Her scent—vanilla and lavender—wraps around me, soothing in ways I cannot explain. Against the forest floor, under branches heavy with shadow, I fall asleep with her close.

A sharp breath and Skia shaking, jolts me awake.

A knife gleams at my throat, its edge reflecting what small light remains from the embers still glowing. Her body tenses in my arms, shallow gasps betraying her panic. Above her, red eyes glow like burning coals. A vampire. Her fangs bared in a cruel smile. Her hair hidden in her cape.

As I stare into the vampire's red eyes, the knife pressing menacingly to my throat, I notice out of the periphery Kain stir at my side. My eyes glance at him as I see him reaching for his sword.

"The princess," she hisses, "has gathered quite the company."

"Touch her and I will burn you from the inside out," I snarl, my teeth grinding together unable to control this feeling of needing to protect her.

"You think you can keep her safe? Then you must not know what lingers here in the dark. You mortal!" She hisses out, holding the knife steady at my throat.

Adrenaline surges. My hand clamps around her wrist. Power erupts from me, light spilling from my hands as I twist the blade free and shove her back. My hand trembles, my body reacting faster than my brain can think and I'm standing, marching toward her. I level the knife at her throat. Hearing Kain's feet coming up behind me. "We have no room for another, leave. Now." I growl out.

Skia rises, but instead of fear, calm radiates from her. I hold the knife steady against her neck. Her voice cracks like thunder inside my skull: *Drop it.*

The command tears through me. My body betrays me, muscles trembling as the knife slips from my hand and falls onto the earth. Fury erupts within me, mixing with confusion. Why would she stop me?

The vampire straightens, crimson eyes never leaving Skia. "As commanding as ever, child of shadows. The Seer was right; there is something buzzing within you. I feel it deep to my core. "she says, as if she did not just threaten us with a knife.

My chest hollows at her words. *The Seer?* I have heard stories of wise ones, prophecies, and magic like gods themselves.

Skia steps forward, her expression unreadable. "Lucile."

The vampire inclines her head, fangs retreating, menace dissolving into something far sharper. Purpose. "I am here to guide you. To keep you alive long enough to fulfill the prophecy. To protect you from the shadows of your father. The Seer has foreseen what comes. Without me, Princess, you will not survive it."

Every nerve in my body screams betrayal, yet Skia's face softens, just barely.

"And who is involved in this prophecy?" I shout, knowing my voice is carrying into the woods, stirring shadows that hide.

I study Skia's face. My heart aches with betrayal. She knows. She has always known.

My jaw clenches, heat burning through me, the ability to hold my light in check becoming thinner by the second. As questions tangle in my chest. What is Skia hiding from me? How will I trust her?

And somewhere deep down, the hollow truth whispers. I have no choice but to trust her.

TWENTY-FIVE
SKIA

Lucile's smirk pulls me, her crimson eyes glowing like embers in the dark. She sits here as if she belongs here, as if the shadows themselves have guided her to my side. Neither ally nor enemy. She is something worse. A tether to the Seer, to the day my world shattered beneath the prophecy's weight. She is the reminder I can never outrun.

The last time I saw her, she stood at the Seer's side in the throne room. My father bellowed his fury, hurling goblets and threats when the Seer dared to proclaim his reign would crumble. Yet Lucile was silent, hooded, strong, her eyes flashing once in defiance before sinking back into shadow. I thought her weak then, insignificant. But looking at her now, tall and unflinching, power carved into the lines of her face, I understand. She has never been weak. She is watching. Waiting.

I walk toward her. My shadows surge, instinctive and venomous.

Ours.

They coil up her spine, curling around her throat in a chokehold of living darkness. "What are you doing here? Why did she send you?" I hiss, shadows tightening with every syllable. I do not know if she is a friend or foe. The distrust is growing. She does not flinch, her eyes glaring. She stands there, fearless, as my shadows stir, wanting more.

End it.

Finish her.

How am I to trust this person that stands in front of me almost mockingly.

My thoughts switch to Meir. All he has lost. His kingdom was attacked by shadows, his people, his land, and his father consumed by them. He sees only another enemy.

Feed.

My shadows twirl her neck, waiting. Lucile's lips curve, her voice a silken taunt. "My dear, while I do enjoy a good choke, you're hardly my taste."

Kain snickers at my side but keeps his fighting stance.

Heat flushes my face. With a growl, I yank my shadows back, there hissing loud in my head, and shove her away with all my strength. She barely moves back. Her laugh follows me, low and knowing.

I feel his eyes burn into the back of my head. The pull gripping me, I turn toward him. I see his eyes, burning with something harsh. Accusations.

Betrayal. He will never trust you again. My shadows bite into my head.

I can't answer him. Not now. Maybe not ever.

"I have asked once. Why are you here, Lucile?" My voice cracks as the shadows whisper their own cruel answers. "Why did the Seer send you?" I continue to push.

She pushes back her hood, revealing braids glinting like ink in the faint starlight, her gaze piercing and unreadable. "Because the path you've chosen has shifted the weave of everything. You need protection. You are where you must be, Skia—and so is he." Her eyes flicked to Meir. His jaw tightens. His silence cuts deeper than any blade.

"What do you mean?" I growl. "The future hangs on every step I take but what if I make the wrong one?" The words spill from my chest.

"You will know soon enough, Skia" she says simply.

Kain steps up, lowering his sword down by his side, "Are those fangs just for show or do you actually use them?"

Lucile smiles, looking at me, "I like this one." Turning her head back to Kain, "If you catch me, I might." she says, giving him a wink.

The distraction of them doesn't help ease my mine. The weight of her words tightens like a chain around my ribs. *The right path?* How could this be right when it left ruin behind me. Chest aching as each thought overtakes, when Meir's father is dead, when his people whisper of war, of getting even because of everything they lost. When every step I take brings Meir deeper into danger? My chest constricts, and the guilt threatens to crush me.

Meir's stare is a wound I cannot close. He sees only betrayal. That I led him here, to Lucile, to a prophecy, a truth he does not want. He cannot know that his presence has changed me—that his light has kindled something in me I thought long dead. That for the first time, I want to be more than a vessel of shadows. I want to be *better*. Do better. Change the world that has gotten so dark. I want to end my father.

But shadows are cruel. They whisper in my mind, their laughter curling sharp and cold: *He will never want us. He will never want you. Your darkness is too much for him.*

Then Lucile interrupts my thoughts, "You all should rest. We have a long day ahead of us tomorrow."

I lie down, trying to calm the shadows. I close my eyes, waiting for his warmth, for the safety of his arms to banish the voices. But when he speaks, his tone is short, his body turning away.

"I'll take first watch." He says, his voice disappearing into the forest.

And then nothing. No warmth. No touch.

The cold sinks into me, outside and in. My shadows snicker in triumph, curling tighter in my chest, until the ache of his absence becomes unbearable. I turn toward him, but he is already gone, his silhouette rigid against the fireless night. My heart fractures in the silence.

TWENTY-SIX
SKIA

12 years ago

The sound of laughter echoes off the stone walls of the castle, too bright, too alive to belong in a place built of onyx and sorrow. It is Raven's laughter, wild, untamed, and daring. I chase after her, my small feet slapping against the cold floor, my shadows swirling at my heels like restless pets trying to keep up.

"Catch me if you can!" she taunts, her voice carrying like music through the dark corridors. Her eyes, bright orange like twin embers, glow in the blue umberflame lining the room, mischief and promise flickering in their depths.

"You're cheating!" I shout, half laughing, half growling, as she darts into a side hall where the light barely reaches.

Her form ripples, blurs, and then she isn't a girl anymore. A sleek black cat darts across the flagstones, tail high, a chirping purr-like sound filling the air.

"That's not fair, Raven!" I groan, stopping short as the surrounding shadows bristle in frustration. "Not everyone can shape shift!"

She shifts back with a grin, sprawling dramatically on the floor. "All's fair when you've got claws." Her voice is alive, a mixture of the girl I know and the animal that lives inside.

I collapse beside her, breathless. "One day, I'll learn how to control them. My shadows. Then you won't get away so easily."

Her smile softens, her orange eyes glowing even brighter as she reaches out and pokes my forehead. "You already have power, Skia. Control them." She breaks off, softer. "You don't need to chase me. You will always have me here." Her words, so simple, etch themselves into my memory, branding my heart with the certainty of her promise.

We lie side-by-side, staring up at the ceiling, the moons lights refracting through the large windows surrounding the room. She whispers, "Do you ever think about leaving? About what's out there?"

I turn my head toward her, giving into the confession, "All the time. But Father will never allow it."

"And if you didn't ask for his permission?" Raven's jaw clenches. Even then, she understands the Shadow King better than I do. She rolls onto her side, her head resting on her hand, voice lower, her orange eyes burning with something fierce and unspoken. "If the world ever turns against you, Skia, I'll be the one still standing at your side. I'll fight them all. I'll never leave you. I promise."

Her vow makes my chest ache with a fierce kind of love, the kind only childhood promises can hold.

And yet, even in the warmth, the air shifts. I feel it before I see it. The way the shadows in the far corner of the corridor grow heavier, thicker, swallowing the torchlight. A shape lingering there, still as stone. Watching.

My father's shadows.

They are everywhere, always listening, always watching. I fear every word I speak in the castle. Everywhere except my room. I turn to Raven. "Let's go to my room," I say as uneasiness settles in my core.

My father, his controlling shadows stir, as we move. His shadows move in irritation. My room is safe, protected against his shadows. A last gift from Ashmore. That night he promised to always protect me, no matter if he is alive or dead.

That is where it all began, the start of the walls crumbling, I knew then that I needed to leave this land.

TWENTY-SEVEN
SKIA

The pack is cold without the warmth of Meir next to me. Morning will come soon, and I need sleep, but the weight on my chest feels like a boulder. Will he ever trust me again? Will he ever accept that I am fated to be his mate? A lifetime with him could mean an eternity of sacrifice, of his wounds becoming mine, mine becoming his, and his breath tied to mine. And yet, if he rejects me, time will stretch into nothing but torment.

The silence presses heavier than any shadow. No crickets, no birds, no wind. The forest's stillness suffocates, a silence too absolute, too intentional. My skin prickles as if unseen eyes crawl over me. Unable to bear it, I get up leaving the pack and wrap my cloak around myself. The air is ice-cold, stealing the heat from my bones.

I sit beside Meir, who fiddles with something in his hand. A golden coin, the Light Land crest flashing in the soft morning light, as he flips it. His jaw is tight. His eyes are unreadable. No words pass between us, yet I cannot stop watching the coin flip in the air, landing in his palm each time. His features hold me captive. His strong jaw, covered with sandy blond facial hair, his blond hair crowning his head tousled by the wind, falling into his piercing blue eyes that consume me whole. A flush spreads down my neck, my heart hammering as if it desires to escape my ribs.

The others stir, the spell between us breaks. I look away from his eyes, doubt still settles in my chest.

We gather everything, ready to start our journey. I quickly scramble onto our horse, Meir right behind me, his arm brushing against my side as he takes the reins. His warmth is comforting, yet his silence feels like an impenetrable barrier.

The Geheimnis Forest deepens. Light breaks through the thick canopy. The air itself seems alive, each tree groaning as though it breathes. The sound of distant howls, snarls, and snapping branches remind us we were not alone. My pulse quickens. Every muscle coils. What are the monsters that hide beyond the trees?

Lucile moves ahead, graceful and silent, leading us deeper. I finally break the suffocating quiet. "Where are you leading us?" My voice cracks. "We follow you with our lives in your hands, yet we know nothing of your intent."

Here voice sounds wise, "There are things you need to see and understand."

The journey feels endless, and silent. It brews within me. The shadows fill my head with doubt.

After hours of riding, the forest shifts. The trees space out, and light breaks through, making my eyes squint. The trees canopy around an entrance. Faint noises bleed into the silence of the last bit of forest. Wagon wheels, laughter, the scent of bread and roasting meats seep into my nose, stirring my stomach with hunger.

Meir reins in sharply. Kain's jaw clenches as they exchange a glance.

Meir leans close, his voice low in my ear. "Tell me, little shadow, are there towns in the Dark Forest?"

I freeze. My heart pounds. The stories of the dangers of the forest flash. "No," I whisper. "No, I don't understand. This shouldn't be here."

And yet, smoke curls above the trees ahead. A village. Alive.

No one returns from the Geheimnis Forest... so how could there be a town within it?

TWENTY-EIGHT
SKIA

The impossible lay before us. I dismount from the horse, feet shuffling on the dirt road. My eyes can't process all that surrounds me.

Through the twisted trees stretch a bustling village, bright with life. Children laugh as they dart between stalls overflowing with wares. Walking the streets, mortals and magicals mingled, their voices rising in a vibrant chorus. The air buzzes with magic, an undercurrent that prickles across my skin like static. This place should not exist, yet it thrives, untouched by the shadows beyond its borders.

The wooden buildings are a mixture of homes and shops. Some two stories, with colorful awnings covering the open doors, inviting in all who walk along the road. The town is so different from anything I have seen in the Light Land and Shadowlands.

I feel jealousy twist inside me at the sight of their smiles, their easy joy. A life untouched by torment, by the weight of prophecy. The shadows are not lingering or watching, the light gives me hope.

People glance our way but do not stop their lives, seemingly accustomed to strangers coming and going. This odd, hidden town accepts us as if we belong. Ahead, the inn beckons, calling to the temptation of a warm bed and warm food. With a soft whisper, I suggest, "Let's get a room, maybe?"

Kain smirks. "One bed for all of us? Cozy." He laughs, breaking through the tension, but Meir's scowl silences him instantly. "Separate rooms, then," he says, with a subtle eye roll as he winks at me.

I laugh despite myself. The sound bubbling out of me unbidden, light against the heavy fog of dread. Kain turns, eyes softening. "Your laughter, it's music after all this silence." His arm drapes over my shoulder, guiding me toward the inn.

"I'll take care of the horses," Meir snaps, the tension clear in his clenched jaw.

When I glance back, Meir's expression is cold, unreadable. My heart twists. No matter how my soul pulls toward him, to him I will always be the enemy. I feel drawn to him, but I am not sure if he feels the same, and I long to see the spark of emotion in his eyes, to decipher the secrets that lie hidden within his guarded heart.

Kain, Lucile and I all wait as Meir works out our accommodation. He comes out, slight frustration still lingering on his face. They have only one room.

The lobby is nothing special. It smells of wood. The windows let light in, highlighting the decor of room. Black and violets coat the room around me. A small black couch sits on one wall with a desk to the side, occupied by the innkeeper, a large man with ginger hair and a mustache and bright blue cat eyes. The innkeeper smiles as we take the stairs. Meir opens the door, tossing the bags inside, his voice sharp, looking at me. "You take the bed. Kain and I will take the floor."

"And Lucile?" I ask, looking at the small room.

"I asked if she needed a room, but she said she had a place to stay." he says.

Meir and Kain leave, allowing me to wash up and change out of the clothes that are covered in dirt. I wonder where Lucile is, she snuck away as we were getting to the inn. How did she know this place? A secret, that must be heavy, as the stories whisper of death, not life in the Geheimnis Forest.

Who else knows of this place?

TWENTY-NINE
SKIA

The air in the room smells of dust. The bed is wedged into the corner, and a table stands next to it with a basin and pitcher of water. Straw sticks out through the thin mattress, creating lumps. The bed was undeniably a bed, even though it was a humble one with mismatched and worn linen and faded red cotton sheets haphazardly arranged.

With a sigh, I grab the small basin on the side table. At least the water is clean. I dip the rough cotton rag, scrubbing the grime from my weary body. My skin sighs in relief. As I glance into the basin, I see the once pristine water has turned murky, swirling with sediment from the demanding journey.

I strip down to my chest wrap and trousers just as the door creaks open. My breath catches. I spin and grab my shirt, clutching it against me, to see Meir standing there.

"Sorry, I was just coming to check on you." His cheeks flushed, blue eyes sweeping over me before locking onto mine.

"Have you heard of knocking, Your Majesty?" I snap, my voice coming out more breathless than I intended.

He steps closer, his gaze burning. The pull between us is screaming and hard to ignore. Behind his eyes I see something, longing. His hand brushes my arm, and then his fingers slide beneath my chin, tilting my face up to his, eyes soft and the ocean pulls me in. My pulse thunders. His nose grazes mine, his breath hot against my skin.

"Your scent is divine heaven," he whispers, voice rough. "Taunting me to jump off the cliff and end it all so I can join you in the heavens."

The words seared through me, my body leaning toward him, craving him. My lips part, pulling him to me.

A sharp knock at the door jolts us apart.

A second knock, louder, insistent. Meir growls low in his throat and wrenches the door open. Kain barges in, Lucile strolling in behind him, arms crossed, a knowing smirk on her lips.

"Sorry for interrupting," Kain mutters, tossing himself onto the bed with his boots still on. The straw bed clouds with dust as he lands.

"Do you mind?" I snap.

He only grins. "Oh Ski, you think there hasn't been worse in this bed?"

I lunge to slap him when Lucile clears her throat. Her crimson eyes glint, sharp and knowing.

"Enough games. ," Lucile interrupts. "We have much to discuss and the forest isn't safe. Some shadows whisper to a larger threat."

Meir steps behind me, pulling me against his chest. "Well, go on then," he insists.

Lucile paces the small floor, shadows clinging to her cloak like smoke. Her presence fills the room, oppressive and commanding.

"I am unsure where to begin," she murmurs, voice sharp as steel. "But I know the Seer wanted you to find this town," she says. "There is much to learn here, knowledge that will give you strength to fight the greatest evil ever to walk in the Shadowlands." Her gaze cuts to me. "Your father. King Morthal."

The name is a curse on her tongue.

I freeze, throat tight, as she goes on. "The Seer fears boundless enemies surrounding you, Skia. And she worries most about what she cannot see. A blackness in her vision, impenetrable, even to her."

Meir interrupts, "And what does that mean?"

Lucile's eyes flick to Meir. "It was not Skia's shadows that killed your father. There is something brewing in the Shadowlands, something we cannot see."

The room is silent. The words crack like thunder.

Meir's entire body goes rigid. His breath quickens, his eyes—those blue eyes I'd drowned in—burn with warring storms of doubt, rage, and something else I can't name.

"She is not your enemy," Lucile finishes. "She is your greatest ally. If you want to win this war, you need her."

"I know she is not my enemy! Her shadows can kill all the Kingdoms of this land, and it will not change how I feel about her," his words a confession

"Lucile, I'm not sure that this has to do with everything? Can you please tell us what we need to know?" I ask.

"This is a great conversation," Kain interjects, laying back on the bed.

Lucile pauses, her gaze lingering on Meir's face as if weighing the depth of his confession. The air in the cramped room thickens. She finally speaks, her tone gentler but still edged with urgency. "Feelings are powerful," she says, "but so is the darkness that threatens us all. You may trust her, but trust must be built on truth, not just emotion."

Kain shifts on the bed, dust swirling once more. "So, what now?" he asks, voice quieter. "If we're up against something even the Seer can't see, where do we begin?"

"We need to go to Lucifis' Lair, where the old gods rest. Each statue a trace of each god's power lingers," she continues. "And tomorrow we will make our way there to get more answers."

Her eyes slide to mine. "Are you going to tell him about the prophecy or do I need to?" Lucile asks.

I look at her, my stomach dropping as she threatens to reveal so much to Meir. She says nothing as the silence eats away at me, her eyes glaring at me. She moves across the room, her cloak sweeping behind her in the movement.

And then she left, shutting the door behind, leaving us choking on the echo of her words. She did not answer questions, leaving more to stir in my mind.

Meir sits by Kain on the bed. The silence stretches, unbearably. Kain's boots tap against the floor, his usual humor absent. I slide down the wall sitting on the floor, frozen, waiting—praying—for Meir to speak.

Kain breaks the awkward silence. "Well, that was cryptic. Is she always like that?"

A small laugh escapes my mouth, "In the few encounters I have had with her, yes, she is."

At last, Meir's eyes meet mine. Softer than before, but still the questions spin in my head.

"Are you going to tell me about the prophecy of my little shadow?" Meir asks, questions sparking on his face.

Enemy. Ally. Fated mate.

Which one am I to him?

I shake my head yes and tell both Kain and Meir of the prophecy.

THIRTY
MEIR

My mind races, a chaotic storm of thoughts swirling in the aftermath of this bizarre event. My focus sharpens on the implications of the revelations, each bit of information a puzzle piece in a larger, terrifying picture.

First, Skia's heritage is confirmed. The whispers and rumors that follow her arrival, hinting at a connection to the Shadowlands, are now undeniable truth. She is not only from the Shadowlands. She is the daughter of the Shadow King, and as she is its rightful heir, a princess born into darkness, destined for it.

Her father killed mine, and for what reason? Did she know? Skia, despite her connection to the Shadowlands and her ominous shadow powers that lurk just below her skin, is not the one who orchestrated his demise. This realization punches a hole in my assumptions, forcing me to reconsider everything I thought I knew about the forces at play.

Finally, the most perplexing element. The prophecy. In a vision, the Seer glimpses Skia's destiny and doom. The fragments Lucile shared are vague, offering no clear guidance, no concrete instructions on how to navigate the treacherous path ahead. As the prophecy foretells, trials and challenges will test our limits, but it provides no clear path.

This isn't a road map; it is a riddle. Uncertainty leaves us adrift, castaways in a desert with no compass and no chart. Deciphering the prophecy's meaning, and understanding its nuances and hidden messages, is necessary for us. We will have to learn to navigate the shadows, to trust in each other, and to forge our own destiny, for no one is going to hand us the answers. We will have to work it out together.

I look over at Ski, and my eyes connect with hers. Why do I feel so drawn to her? Her eyes call to me like a lush meadow. I am lost in her stare, her piercing green eyes, a field I long to stay in forever. I feel myself falling into her—

An uncomfortable cough interrupts my thoughts, and I look at Kain awkwardly in the weird silence. He shakes his head and looks at me, accepting me and understanding. "We should all get ready for sleep. I'll lay my pack over here, and then, Skia, you can have the bed. Meir, you set your pack up right there in front of the bed." He looks at Skia.

He digs in his backpack and hands me some dried meat. Skia lifts her eyebrows. "You mean to tell me you're going to eat dried meats when there is a whole town full of shops and adventures to have?"

Grabbing her things, she turns to the two of us. "We need a proper meal. We don't know how long we'll be here and might as well have a full stomach." She crosses her arms, waiting for us to respond.

I look at Kain. "She has a point. We might as well get a meal."

I gather my things and walk to the door. Kain sighs but follows behind. "Where do you suggest?" Kain asks, the excitement growing behind his eyes.

She smiles, a genuine expression I rarely see. "I think I saw a tavern close to here when we came into town."

She walks, her pace brisk and determined. Kain and I exchange a look, then fall into step behind her, the promise of warmth and sustenance drawing us forward.

A vibrant tapestry of life unfolds on the streets outside. The air thrums with the movement of creatures and mortals, their smells and sounds intermingling. They coexist and thrive in this town. As we walk, the sun has dropped low on the horizon. It's setting..

I stop walking and watch the changing colors of the sky. Somehow, the sun sets in the middle between the dark and the light, and the darkness only lasts for a little while. It was a delightful fusion, oranges, purples, and pinks tinting the sky.

My first sunset, a breathtaking spectacle of fiery oranges and deep purples, unlike the light of my homeland. Some darkness gathers around the setting sun, as if the darkness hugs the light from the sky. Together, the combination of the two is a beautiful masterpiece.

I feel her beside me, watching the sunset with me. "It is as if the darkness craves the light. With the shadows, there is also light." She glances at me. "The perfect duo," she says, her voice soft as a feather.

"I think there is a pub over there. Why don't we try to find something to eat there?" Kain says, grabbing my attention.

A sign hanging outside the building reads, Hopa, in large letters. The people enter laughing, everything about this place is charged with hope.

We walk through the door, and the place is full. The chatter fills the pub. The smells are a mixture of ale and cooking food. It feels warm, and a small fire crackles in the fireplace in the center of the room. The bartender smiles as he sees us enter. He is tall, his skin dark and his eyes gold. He wipes the counter with a rag as he converses with an interesting creature. It is a small woman, though she is half doe, her feet small hooves and antlers between her long copper hair. A lone, unoccupied table sits in the pub's far corner. We work our way through the maze of patrons and sit. The room is an eclectic mix. Mortals, vampires, and who knows what all sit together, laughing and having conversations.

We call over to the bartender for three ales. He calls for someone to bring us our drinks. The barmaid's shoulders sprouted two arms on either side. She set our mugs on the table along with a bowl of pistachios. She smiles. Her eyes, her eyes a shocking yellow, sparked and crinkled at the corners, contrasting sharply against her soft blue skin.

"New here?" she asks.

"No, do you get visitors often?" I ask.

She smiles knowingly. She doesn't believe him for a moment. "Mostly from the towns bordering us, but the occasional stranger finds their way here." she says. "What can I get you to eat?" she asks, putting one of hands on her waist.

I look around and see a small menu behind the bar. "Rabbit stew." I say and Skia and Kain order the same. She leaves us.

"This place is unlike anything I have ever seen." I see the stark contrast between here and my home. The excitement that fills the air and the laughter that rings in my ears make me feel at ease, almost safe.

"I feel like it is not far from the Light Lands. We are pretty cheerful people." Kain argues, glancing up as the barmaid brings us steaming plates of food that look and smell delicious. I pick up my spoon and stir the stew, bits of carrot and potatoes rising to the top. I take a bite and it is the best thing I have ever eaten. The flavors dance on my tongue filling my mouth.

"So, little shadow, is that scowl meant for me, the stew or Kain?" I ask.

Her eyes look up to me squinting, "You." A hint of a smile starts to bloom on her lips.

"Ah, I see. Do you always look at the world as a battle you have already lost?" I question.

"Better to expect loss than be surprised by it," she says scooping stew into her mouth.

Her eyes meet mine, "Or, you could expect hope instead. Know you aren't fighting the battle alone."

Her eyes drop, heat rising to her cheeks, "I fight all my battles alone, just me and my shadows."

A tug pulls at my chest, an echo of her loneliness, I reach my hand under her chin, lifting her head. "Little shadow, with me you do not have to fight the battles alone."

Her green eyes linger, and I feel myself lost in them. "You're insufferable," she whispers, longing dancing behind her eyes.

"And yet, if I were gone, you would miss me, would you not?" I wink, returning to my food.

Laughter, chatter, and clinking glasses fill the cozy pub's atmosphere, distracting me from my thoughts. The patrons seem like a diverse group. Locals sharing stories, travelers seeking respite, and magical beings blending with mortals in harmony.

For the first time, I see what could be. Light and shadow together, thriving. A spark of hope flickers in my chest.

While Skia and I have been talking, Kain has been flirting with the barmaid every time she passes our table. Their gazes linger. He whispers crude promisies, laughing at his own wit, his hands too eager.

He catches my eye and my disapproving frown, "Do you two think you're the only ones to have fun?" he asks.

"Would you rather I flirt with your little shadow Meir?" Kain asks as the barmaid walks away looking back at him biting her smile.

My mind races to imagines of his hand playing along Skia's leg, or his lips kissing hers. My mind throws these thoughts at me, a simple sentence lighting a fire within me that I did not know I possessed.

Suddenly, I feel the light burn within me. The air thrums with magic awakening my own. The magic I try to bury inside me. I look down and see light seeping from my fingers. I jump up, making my way through the crowded pub.

Kain's voice calls after me, but I don't stop.

The crisp air hits me like a blessing. I gulp it in, desperately, trying to calm the storm inside me. I look around for distractions, trying to push the light down.

The street is alive with color and chaos. Lanterns glow in hues of sapphire and crimson. Their enchanted flames shift like restless spirits. Vendors shout. Their wares shimmer with faint traces of magic. Silks woven with threads of moonlight, potions bubbling with impossible hues, meats roast on spits that smoke with golden sparks.

And still, even here, even surrounded by wonder, my thoughts return to her. Skia. Her shadows. Her eyes. The feeling that I am bound to her by something deeper than fate.

As my eyes take in all around me, that is when I see her.

Lucile.

She leans casually against a weathered wooden wall of the pub outside. A slender pipe rests between her fingers, smoke curling into the air like whispered secrets. Her eyes are closed, serene, until the weight of my stare makes her lashes lift.

Blood-red irises gleam in the moonlight. And she smiles, slow and menacing.

"I feel you staring," she murmurs, her voice soft and melodic, a thread of silk weaving into the night. "So, tell me, Meir … are you ready to ask the questions, or will you keep pretending you don't already know the answers?"

THIRTY-ONE
SKIA

My spoon stirs the remaining stew in my bowl, I watch the spoon turn, turn, and turn. Meir left so quickly. He is upset, and I just sit here denying the truth of how we both feel for each other and the pull that tugs at my chest to be closer to him. I want nothing more than to follow him. To finally push past all these feelings that are consuming me. The feeling of his arms around me and his hands against my skin. I want it. All of it.

Yet here I sit, a prisoner of my own making, ignoring the insistent pull in my chest, the desperate longing to follow him. He is a beacon, a sunbeam that has somehow stumbled into my world, and I, a creature of the deepest shadows, don't deserve the warmth he radiates.

I feel a profound self-inflicted darkness, a crushing weight. My darkness taints me. My father, the architect of so much suffering, is the evil that robs him of his father, a loss that still echoes in the quiet moments between us. The realization of my unworthiness settles over me like a shroud. I am unworthy of a mate, of companionship, of the simple joy of belonging.

I miss Raven, my best friend. Someone to talk to. Someone to help me work out the thoughts that are too heavy on my mind.

I feel a simmering frustration with fate, a bitter resentment for the cruel, cosmic joke it seems to play. How could a creature born of the shadows, a being whose essence was woven from darkness and regret, find solace, let alone a mate, in the radiant light he embodies? The contrast is too stark; the gulf between us is too vast. I am utterly unworthy of something so intrinsically good.

I lift my face to Kain's eyes. Weirdly familiar eyes. Gold embers. His eyes flit to mine while he flirts with the server. He whispers in her ear, his hands brushing against her bare shoulders, before he returns to the table and takes his seat.

"She's free for the rest of the night and has asked me to come over." he smiles.

"Don't get me wrong, love," Kain says to me, his voice a silken drawl that is both playful and sincere. "It is tempting to stay the night in the room with the two of you, but if I could find someone to keep me warm tonight versus lying on a mat on the floor, I'm going to take it." He winks at me, but something else stirs behind his eyes. Just for a moment, a spark of something I can't decipher, before he returns to the female.

I speak, the words a desperate attempt to distract myself from the turmoil within. "What is Meir's backstory? How did you two meet?" The question hangs in the air, a fragile thread of curiosity in the face of overwhelming self-doubt.

He raises a sculpted eyebrow, a hint of amusement playing on his lips. "His father and mine were friends, or well, my father worked for him. We grew up together, side-by-side, through trials and triumphs. He's as close as anyone could get to family. Ultimately, he is like my brother."

"Well, have fun," I say as he walks away.

Brother. The word lodges sharp in my chest. Meir is like his brother. Raven is like my sister. Or at least, she is supposed to be. The weight of that thought sits like a stone in my gut, reminding me that chosen bonds can be the sharpest blades when they break.

THIRTY-TWO
MEIR

I sense a pull toward her, as if she possesses the answer to a question I did not ask yet. I walk closer. The smugness on her face is infuriating, but here I am, ready to ask the hard questions that gnaw at me.

"I want the answers," I demand.

Her eyes meet mine, and she reaches for my arm. The moment her fingers brush my skin, the world tilts and suddenly I'm not where I just was.

A blinding light, then nothing.

When my vision clears, I stand in a field of carnage. The air is thick with the metallic tang of blood and the acrid sting of smoke. Bodies, twisted and broken, lie scattered across the muddy ground. The clash of steel and the guttural cries of the dying still ring in the air as if the battle ended only moments ago.

Then, through the chaos, I see her.

Skia.

Emerald eyes cut through the haze, locking onto mine. She stands in armor spattered with blood, her jaw set, her presence commanding. Light and shadow coiled around her like living things. My hand lifts on its own, desperate to reach her, to anchor myself to something solid amidst the nightmare.

The world tears away again.

Now, I see her beaten and blood dripping from her face. Chains bind her wrists to a dungeon wall etched with marks that pulse with sickly light. Shadows writhe and spill toward her body like smoke choking the air. Her skin is bruised, her face bloodied, but her eyes—gods, her eyes—still burn with a defiance that hollows me out. A drip of water echoes like a clock counting down. Somewhere in the darkness, claws scrape on stone. I try to move toward her, but I am frozen, forced to watch her break. My chest caves, breaths strangle in my throat.

Another rip, and Skia is before me again. Close. So close. Her smile glows warm, impossibly tender. I can feel the coolness of her skin against mine, the way my warmth answers it. Her gaze fixes on me, as if the rest of the world has ceased to exist.

"Mine," she whispers, her voice a silken promise that pierces me to my core.

I want to stay here forever.

But the vision shatters.

I fall to my knees on the road, the weight of it crashing into me. My stomach lurches, bile burning my throat. My palms press against the dirt as I try to steady myself, but the echo of her voice—*mine*—still rings in my ears, binding itself to my bones.

Lucile crouches in front of me, her expression unreadable, as though she's seen this a thousand times before. Her red eyes glimmer in the half-light.

"Your future," she says simply. Her words feel less like an answer and more like a sentence.

Before I can demand more, she steps back. The shadows cling to her form and swallow her whole, leaving only the faintest curl of perfumed smoke in the air. Gone.

I stay frozen in place, staring at the spot where she vanished. My pulse thunders, my hands tremble, and my thoughts tangle in a snarl of fear and hunger.

Was this truly my future? Am I meant to love her, to lose her, to watch her torn apart by the very shadows she commands? Is my kingdom destined to burn while I reach for a woman born to ruin me?

The battlefield, the chains, her whisper—it all burns behind my eyes. And despite the horror, despite everything, one truth cuts sharper than the rest.

Even covered in blood, even wrapped in darkness… she still pulls me closer.

And I fear, no, I know, that I will follow her into ruin.

THIRTY-THREE
SKIA

The door of the pub and Mier walks in. He looks peaky, his face pale and drawn, a stark contrast to the jovial atmosphere of the pub. I watch as he zigzags through the crowd, navigating the throng of bodies with practiced ease, finally returning to our table. Kain already left with the server, and I am enjoying the vibrant scene unfolding around me. Even as the outside world grows darker, the interior of the pub becomes more alive, fueled by the energy of the gathering. The people grow louder, their voices blending into a harmonious roar, and the pub buzzes with tangible energy. A small band crammed into a corner near the fireplace launches into a lively tune. The music, a familiar melody, prompts a few brave souls to dance and sing in the limited space, their movements a joyful celebration of the moment. I smile at the scene that unfolds before me, a picture of camaraderie and simple glee.

    I yearn for many things, especially the simple freedom to laugh and savor life. The darkness of the Shadowlands cling to every corner of the land I visit, a suffocating presence that steals the light and the joy. The weight of becoming the next dark ruler has never intrigued me, the prospect of wielding such power a burden rather than a prize. I want my land to have freedom, for its people not to live in fear, to experience the same carefree joy that I see in this humble pub. We feel liberated, yet omnipresent shadows still consume dissenters, a constant reminder of the darkness that lurks beneath the surface. But here, in this place, the air feels lighter. The people don't feel afraid. Their laughter rings out without hesitation, and their faces are open and unguarded. It gives me hope for the future, a glimmer of light in the pervasive darkness, a sign that perhaps, one day, such joy can be commonplace.

    Meir sits down across from me, his presence immediately filling the small space at the table in the dimly lit tavern. "Kain wandered off?" he asks, his brow furrowing with a touch of concern. I meet his gaze and nod.

Seeing him up close, the way the flickering candlelight dances across his features make it difficult to ignore the feelings that are, against my will, yearning deep inside me. These feelings are a dangerous mix of admiration and affection. The ale I have been sipping is not helping. Instead of easing the tension, it amplifies everything, as the world blurs at the edges. I feel a strange, unexpected sense of bliss sitting here with him, a sense of peace that I am not sure I deserve. I, a creature of shadows and darkness, and he, a beacon of light, yet here, at this moment, the dichotomy doesn't seem to matter. I feel a spark of something I didn't feel in a long time, a genuine flicker of happiness.

Before I allow the feeling to spread further, before I get lost in the intoxicating warmth of his presence, I decide it is probably a good idea to return to the inn and try to sleep. I am not sure where Lucile is taking us, what trials or tribulations await us on the road ahead, but I know I need to rest and be ready for whatever lay ahead. I briefly wonder if Meir feels anything similar. Does he see anything other than a monster when he looks at me?

"Where did Kain even go?" he asks as I push myself away from the table, the rough wood banging against my leg. Meir's brow furrows as he looks at me, his expression a mixture of concern and amusement. I sit back down. My cheeks burn with embarrassment.

"You must enjoy this." I say through gritting teeth.

"What is that, little shadow?" He says, his voice low and his eyes locking on mine.

"Seeing me in pain." The words snap from my mouth.

"No, little shadow, I swear to you, I will burn through the world, before I ever let anyone lay a hand on you." The muscles in his jaw are ticking as he says every word. He ignites a fire inside me.

The tavern is emptying, with the late-night revelers trickling out into the narrow, dirt streets. "I'm going back to the inn. Kain found different company so he won't be coming back to the room tonight." I smirked, grabbing my heavy woolen cloak from the back of the chair. The firelight dances across its worn fabric, casting long shadows on the floor. "I'm heading back. Promise me you'll be careful, alright?"

He grins, a flash of white in the dim light of the sputtering oil lamps hanging above the tables. "Always. Now go get some rest. You look like you could use it."

With a final, lingering glance, I turn and walk toward the door, the raucous music, and boisterous laughter fading behind me as the cool night air washes over me, carrying the scent of wood smoke. The rhythmic thrum of the city, the distant shouts of drunkards and the clatter of horses' hooves, provides a familiar soundtrack to my solitary journey. Sleep's promise and a chance for quiet escape beckoning.

But as I pull the cloak tighter around me, the shadows along the alley shift, too deliberate, too alive. A shiver crawls up my spine. For an instant, I swear I see the gleam of orange eyes before the dark swallows them whole. The words of the Seer whisper through my mind.

My chest tightens. Am I running toward salvation, or straight into betrayal?

Either way, the shadows are watching.

Waiting.

THIRTY-FOUR
SKIA

No matter how I shift, the hay jabs at my skin, refusing me comfort. Sleep will not come. I lie in the scratchy bed, listening to Meir's steady breaths. My mind is a cage of frantic wings, a bird thrashing itself bloody against the bars of anxiety. When he had left during dinner, I wondered if he'd ever return, or if he'd ride back to his kingdom and forget me entirely.

The room's chill cut like a winter wind, a cruel contrast to the forest floor where I'd once slept so easily in his warmth. After hours of tossing, I rise and slip down beside him, lifting the edge of his meager blanket. His arm wraps instinctively around me, pulling me close. The heat of him, the rough circle his fingers trace against the back of my hand, melts the tension in my body. He is awake, but he does not push me away.

The rhythmic touch lulls me, my eyes growing heavy. I try to fight the tide of sleep, desperate to hold on to this moment, but warmth conquers me. My body sinks into his, and darkness takes me.

When I wake, his breath is soft against my neck, steady, and grounding. His arm still wraps around my waist. His head tucks into the crook of my shoulder, and for a moment I let myself believe—dangerously believe—that this will last. My veins erupt as his touch shifts, his hands trailing over me with slow reverence. His lips brush the back of my neck, trailing kisses from my ear to my shoulder. My body betrays me, a soft moan escaping and arching into him, surrendering. My soul whispers his name like a prayer.

Bam.

The door bangs open.

Kain.

Meir exhales sharply and pushes up on one elbow. "Ever heard of knocking?" His tone was edged steel.

I scramble, tugging my shirt down, heat flooding my face as Kain leans lazily against the doorframe. He takes us in—the tangle of limbs, Meir's bare chest, the flush still clinging to my skin. A wolfish grin spreads across his face.

"Well, well. I didn't mean to interrupt. Want me to step out and give you a moment?" His sneer lingers as he crosses the room and sprawls onto the bed with his boots still on. "Glad I wasn't the only one who found company last night. The difference is—mine was in an actual bed." He says with a wink.

His laughter grates, smug and unrelenting. I shoot to my feet, snatching up my boots and pack.

"I'll be outside getting the horse ready," I snap, storming from the room. The slam of the oak door shakes the frame as I stomp into the hall, find the stairway and leave the inn.

The chill outside cuts sharper than any blade. Sitting on the porch steps, I shoved my boots on with stiff fingers. The town is quiet, That was when I see her.

Lucile.

She stands leaning against the wall, her braided hair falling down the length of her back. The sun makes her dark skin glow. She takes a long drag on the pipe in her hand And exhales slowly, the smoke curling into the air. The earthy smell wafts to me.

Our eyes meet. She smiles.

"I know you worry about the future," she says quietly. "But I see him there by your side. But not all who walk beside you do so out of loyalty. I think it's important for you to remember that Skia."

Her words lodge in my chest like a shard of glass. "What do you mean?" The questions run through my mind. I walk toward her, she offers her pipe to me and I decline.

"Who can I not trust? Can you tell me?" I ask. "Please?" I plead.

She only shrugs. "I do not know who betrays you, only that you cannot trust everyone around you. The gods have not granted me with all the sight yet."

"You can also see the future?" I question. "I thought only Seers have the sight?"

"Yes, the next Seer gains their sight when the other Seer is close to their end. It can be years or a few months, but each Seer trains her replacement." She states.

I try to process it — the Seer — she has been in my life for as long as I can remember. She would come to the castle often, giving my father prophecies.

"Oh, and what happens when they reach their end? What does that mean?" I question.

"They are dead." She states a fact, devoid of emotion, or any concern for a loss of life.

I don't know what to say, every word flees from my mind. I grab my things, feeling like I have too much knowledge but also not enough. The frustration builds and I push it down.

"I'm going to the horses," I say as I pass her.

The scent of lavender smoke clings to her as she lets me go by.

THIRTY-FIVE
SKIA

I run my hand through the horse's mane that I have gotten to know over the past few days. Her steadiness calms the racing thoughts in my head. Leaning my head against her, I run my hand back and forth and shut my eyes.

Doubt claws at me, an icy dread spreading through my limbs. Meir's love, a beacon I deem unattainable, feels like a warm embrace I don't deserve. He is the embodiment of light, a stark contrast to the suffocating darkness I know so well.

The kingdom of my upbringing, a place where whispers of my inadequacy echoed endlessly, still holds me captive. Can I ever escape the years of feeling insufficient, and finally, be enough?

The possibility flickers. Can I deserve Meir's love? A warm glow against the chill of my past, a hopeful ending to a life steeped in shadow. He is the bright beacon beckoning from the stifling, dark passage I have struggled through. The shadows are heavy; they weigh on my mind.

They make me both strong and weak. Using them, I feel the last embers of my humanity dwindle, a chilling void spreading within. Though the shadows press close, a suffocating darkness, they do not devour me. They are a constant icy presence, a familiar chilling companion.

They coil in my stomach, an icy knot that tightens with each fleeting moment of self-doubt. My breath hitches in my chest, and my muscles tense, as if bracing for a blow that might never come. A tremor runs through my fingertips as I contemplate the impossible. Deserving Meir's affection.

For a moment, Raven's childhood vow echoes in my mind — *I'll never leave you, Skia.* The memory burns like a ghost against my chest. I miss her and I have so much to tell her. I regret leaving her behind, not knowing what my father did to her to get information from her.

I hear a sound come from the corner of the stable, the shadows stir. For a heartbeat, I swear silver eyes gleam, watching, weighing, waiting. My mind plays tricks on me. My father's silence presses down even across distance, his presence an invisible chain I can never quite shake.

I don't notice the footsteps coming up behind me. I am so lost in thought, but I feel his hands wrap around my waist, his body leaning against mine. He intertwines his hands with mine and embraces my body. He puts his head in the nook of my neck, and he takes a deep breath. He smells of petrichor and sandalwood. I sigh, the air thick with his scent, knowing this is what I want.

"Little shadow," he whispers, his voice soft and deep. "I want to deny this pull to you, but I can't anymore. The scent of your hair, the curve of your form against my hand — all my senses scream you are mine. You are more than just a woman, more than a princess of shadows. You are mine." He confesses.

His voice, a low rumble that vibrates against my back, sends a shiver down my spine.

"You speak as if it is so simple. As if I can just belong to you and not lose myself. Do you even know what it costs me to believe you?" I say. "I am nothing but shadows, why would you want me, broken and barely holding it all together?"

"Don't. Don't ever believe that of me. Your pain is the only thing in this world I cannot endure," he says.

"And yet," I sigh, "It follows me, consumes me."

A single tear, warm against my cheek, traces a path. He turns me around to look into my eyes. He holds me there, his concern covering his face. My whole life is a search, a silent yearning for a connection I'm not sure exists.

Then, standing before me, is the answer, the missing piece, the very reason for my being. This is exactly what I have waited for my whole life to hear, and maybe I am the princess of shadows, cloaked in the secrets and darkness of the world, and he is the king of light, a beacon of hope and joy, but together, intertwined, we are so much more than the sum of our separate strengths.

I look up, tilting my chin, and meet his gaze. His blue eyes, the color of the endless sky, hold the power and beauty of a crashing ocean, a depth I could easily drown in. A dizzying sensation of falling, of losing myself completely, overwhelms me. His face is so close, so overwhelmingly present, I can feel the brush of his stubble against my skin, a tantalizing friction that sends shivers down my spine. Our breaths quicken, a shared, heated rush of air.

The world narrows, the periphery fading, until there is only him, only the burning need between us. His mouth nears, and then, finally, his lips meet mine. A spark ignites, a wildfire that consumes everything. His lips move, a gentle exploration, an unspoken question lingering behind his kiss. I open to him, his tongue, a velvet invitation, glides against mine, a perfect dance of longing and discovery. Our tongues intertwine, a silent conversation of souls, a merging that feels inevitable, predestined. My body sways, the strength in my legs failing me, and my arms tighten around him, pulling me closer, desperate to meld, to become one. He lifts my legs and I wrap them around his waist. His hands move, exploring my body. My hair catches in his hands, securing me and pulling me further into the kiss, which whispers of eternity.

It feels like an eternity in those fleeting moments, lost in the blissful oblivion of his touch.

He breaks the kiss resting his forehead against mine, his breath catching. "You are mine." He pauses, then continues, "And I am yours. Shadows and light, we face whatever comes. A team forged in ways no one could predict." A soft sigh escapes him. "You are everything. My soul sings for you. All of you — the darkness, the past, present, and future — I accept it all."

He kisses my forehead, a soft, reverent touch, and my eyes flutter closed. Surrounded by magic, I am thankful that fate brings us together. In the silence of my heart, I whisper a prayer of gratitude to the gods above.

A cough from behind Meir abruptly pulls us back into the present, breaking the spell that had enveloped us moments before. Kain stands nearby, a broad grin on his face as he claps his hands together once in amusement.

"I am glad to see that both of you have finally made it official," he says with a hearty laugh, his voice carrying a note of genuine happiness for us. Though the words are light, they serve as a reminder of the journey still ahead.

Kain quickly shifts the mood to practicality, urging us onward. "We should probably get a move on with the trip; it will be a long one. We arrive sooner if we leave sooner, which helps complete our goal." His suggestion is met with a shared understanding. The path before us will not wait, and our purpose calls us forward.

The crisp morning air nips at my exposed cheeks as I nod in agreement, my gaze locks on the dense, foreboding forest that borders the edge of town.

"The journey will take most of today, we should arrive mid-morning tomorrow." Lucile's words hang in the air as she walks into the stable. "There's a town along the way, but we'll need to camp. No inns." She looked at Meir and me, a smile playing on her lips. "Are you ready?"

Together, Meir and I mount our horse, the familiar sway of its gait a comforting presence amidst the growing tension. We move toward the town's outskirts. The dirt street slowly transforms into a muddy track that leads straight into the woods. Today, we explore the endless Dark Forest, teeming with more secrets than we can even begin to anticipate. The shadows of the trees dance and shift, casting an ethereal glow on the path ahead, and I can't help but feel a prickle of unease crawl up my spine. The forest seems to watch us.

THIRTY-SIX
SKIA

The forest closes in around us, a canopy weaving a ceiling of shadow and light. Sunlight fractures through leaves, sprinkling light across the path. The hooves of the horses thud against the damp earth.

The air is cool, sparking a shiver that runs through me. I shiver slightly as the air grows cooler. Meir wraps his arms around me, pulling me against his warmth.

Kain tugs at his reins, leaning back in his saddle with a grin. "If one of you gets us lost out here, don't expect me to spear us a feast. I barely know which mushrooms kill you and which don't. They never taught us those things in Luminaria."

Lucile walks ahead of us, using her shadows to fade in and out going along the path. She smiles at Kain, her fangs sharp. "Then I suppose you'll have to starve because while you mortals need food, I've had my fill."

Lucile glances over her shoulder, her eyes glinting as she moves. "Try to keep up, Kain. The forest isn't forgiving to those who dawdle."

Kain rolls his eyes, but his tone is light. "I'm just saying, if we run into trouble, I hope you're not expecting me to wrangle wild beasts."

Meir tightens his grip around me, whispering, "It's not the beasts I worry about—it's the things you can't see."

Lucile's laughter is soft, almost haunting. "That's the thrill, isn't it? Not knowing what's waiting around the bend."

I swallow, trying to mask my nerves. "Let's just hope whatever's waiting is friendly."

Kain clicks his tongue. "Friendly or not, we stick together. That's how we get through the Dark Forest."

Lucile smiles, her voice dropping low. "Agreed. One wrong step, and you might find the shadows have teeth."

The forest still has so much I don't know about it. As we ride, the air grows heavier, and I feel like there is constantly someone watching. The unease makes me shake, and Meir whispers in my ear, "You okay?"

I shake my head. "I just feel like something is wrong, or off. I'm sure it's just the Dark Forest. I remember being told stories about the monsters that linger here, who feast on children for breakfast." The stories Ashmore told me.

"What's it like in the Shadowlands?" Meir asks, running a hand through my hair.

"Dark," I laugh.

I feel his chest vibrate with his laughter. "You don't say, my little shadow. But really what is it like?" His question lingers, I'm not sure how I can answer the question.

The sound of the horse's hooves fill the air. "I have a best friend. Her name is Raven. She's my Kain. We grew up together for as long as I can remember. Her mother died when she was young."

Meir's hand pauses, gentle in my hair. "She sounds special," he says quietly, letting the horse slow as he waits for me to finish.

I nod, a soft smile tugging at my lips. "She is. We looked out for each other, especially after her mom was gone. The Shadowlands don't make things easy, but Raven always made me feel like I belonged."

Meir hums thoughtfully, his eyes on the path ahead. "I like that. That you found someone like that."

I glance over my shoulder at the others. "And now ... you have me."

He smiles, and this time it reaches his eyes. "Yeah. I think I'm lucky."

The silence between us is comfortable now, the rhythm of hooves and the hush of the Geheimnis Forest wrapping around us. Meir squeezes my hand, and I lean closer, letting the quiet settle. For a moment, it feels like even the shadows are watching over us, gentle instead of menacing.

"Thank you," Meir whispers, his voice so low it's almost lost to the forest. "For sharing. For being here."

I squeeze his hand in return. "Always."

"Hey guys, there's something strange up here," Lucile calls out. Meir and I look toward her and see her just up the path. Meir shakes the reins, and the horse canters forward.

Kain isn't far behind us. Lucile stands there; her horror-filled face leaves me feeling hollow. At the bottom of the trees, blood seeps onto the forest floor, making the path muddy. Blood bled from all the trees along the path.

I feel a cool drip on my hand and look to see a red dot dripping down. I look up and the forest, with all of its limbs, rains blood.

"We need to go," I say, the unease growing. "Can you transport Kain?" I ask Lucile.

Lucile nods. "I'm going to transport us up the path."

She says a spell the shadows begin to stir as she speaks the words, ancient and powerful. As she touches Kain's horse, I call upon my shadows. As the shadows close in, I look up. I see the tree limbs reaching toward us, their blood leaking all over my face and I feel Meir grow tense as finally we are swallowed by the shadows and taken away.

We followed our shadows down the path, leaving the place we had just been. The path we'd walked vanished behind us, and I was relieved to have Lucile's abilities.

"Oh, gods," Kain bellows as we move the horses forward. "How do you do that? I feel like my head is going to split open."

"It's transporting; it takes some getting used to," I say, my mind still spinning. "What was that?" I question Lucile.

"The bloodwood," she states. My mind races through all the things I have ever read of the Dark Forest. There was some mention of the people who went in not coming back, but that didn't answer the question of how cities thrive here.

"Bloodwood?" I question.

I glance at Kain. He looks pale and slight sheen of sweat covers his skin.

"You okay, Kain?" Meir asks, looking over to him.

"Peachy," Kain replies.

"Why were the trees bleeding?" I press. "The books always said the trees feasted, but I never thought that meant they actually did." The questions tumble through my brain, and I try to recall anything and everything that I have read about the dark forest.

"The bloodwood is linked to our magic, in a way the forest is the mother of all our magic," Lucile says, and her face is blank of any expression. As if she hadn't answered a question that had been on my mind for years.

"I thought our magic was tied to the old gods." I recalled the paragraph that I'd read hundreds of times.

"In a way, but all life is born from the earth. When the gods came to this realm, there was nothing and they each had a part in the creation of our lands."

"Born from Niaxias, the shadows formed, covering the earth until Lucifis brought forth his light, the other gods and goddesses added each element, earth, air, and fire. Each mortal was born from the sacred passage." she says.

"For years the earth gave life and helped make each mortal stronger, slowly the forest gave the mortals more, powers grew and soon war broke out because the mortals craved more. Then the lands separated and feared the Geheimnis Forest and the power that it had. The Geheimnis Forest grew angry. All magic came from the forest, but the mortals grew greedy, wanting more power and when those mortals betrayed Geheimnis, it wanted back the magic it had given." she says, as she disappears into the shadows, weaving in and out.

The story tosses around in my brain. This was never in any book that I had read, and I felt like more questions clawed at me for answers.

"Is this a story that you know?" I ask Meir and Kain. "This was not in any books that I read."

I feel Meir tense. "No, this is not a story that we were taught either."

The air fills with silence. How much of our history has been changed, and we are unaware of the lies we were fed?

THIRTY-SEVEN
SKIA

After hours of riding through the forest, we came upon a stream and stopped to water the horses and filling our water skins. Though smaller, it has a mixture of magic and mortals. I marvel at how things here harmonize and flourish, while the light and shadow lands teeter on war. The towns give me hope that if I can just get each land to see the truth, we can all thrive and be one. Though that will bring on a different war altogether, the watchers and hunters will never allow such a thing to happen.

"What's the reason for the Watcher and the Hunters? I ask.

Lucile looks up. "They protect the mortals and the magic." Her voice trails off as if she's leaving something out.

I turn. "What are they really for, Lucile? The blood-trees, the magic, the stories. All I have been fed are lies. So what are they really there for?" I demand.

"The Watchers are the guards for the Light Lands…" she rises, turning toward me, her red eyes piercing me. "The Hunters … work for your father."

The air leaves my lungs, my body crushed by a mountain of rocks. Im at a loss. I turn away, ending the conversation; nothing is going to help. I am a cup, overflowing with emotions.

***

The small town lacks an inn and we make camp just outside the town. We ignite a fire and roast the rabbit Kain captured earlier. The day silences conversation.

I notice the more time Meir spends with me, the more his body language changes. His hands linger on my back, brush my leg, or touch my hair as if he is desperate for a connection. The fire crackles, and the smell of the roasting rabbit wafts in the air, making my stomach growl.

The odd thing about being in the Geheimnis Forest is the eerie feel of the surrounding air. No wind stirs. The entire forest is completely silent other than the fire and the brief movements we make.

"Well, today was eventful." Kain says finally breaking the silence. He is lying on the ground, one knee bent, twirling a branch through his fingers.

As the flames dance, casting long shadows that stretch and twist with the flickering light, I watch Meir.

"Yeah," Meir laughs, brushing his golden blond hair back. Strands glisten in the fire making it look like pure gold. He sits a little apart from the fire, his gaze fixed on me. His eyes, usually bright with a playful light, seem clouded with something I cannot quite decipher.

I try to focus on the task at hand, helping Lucile arrange our meager supplies. But I keep catching Meir's gaze. The way he watches me, each gaze making my stomach flutter, an ache growing. I gravitate toward him, each touch craving another. The tension between us is a palpable thing, a silent current that runs beneath the surface of our shared silence.

Between Meir and I the silence amplifies the unspoken words, the aching need to touch, to link legs. The gentle touch of his hand on mine goes with his offering of roasted rabbit. His eyes linger on my lips as I devour a bite. The warm meat is too hot in my mouth. He sits behind me, bracing on knee against my side, and I lean on his leg.

We finish eating and lie intertwined on our packs. His hands wind across my waist and neck, his fingers weaving through my hair. He kisses my head. I pull away and look into his eyes. I touch my hand to his face, his stubble rough under my soft skin. I bring my lips to his, brushing my mouth to his. I linger there, a soft kiss, his hand wrapping in my hair. I open my lips, parting his. My tongue dancing along his. His subtle traces of my lips make the heat from my soul ignite.

A cough comes from across the fire. "I wish I had those shadow powers of yours, Lucile, because I'd really like to be anywhere but right here right now." He interrupts.

"I agree," Lucile chirps.

My body is still aching, I lean my head against his chest, nestling into his neck, his heartbeat a steady thump in my ear, a lullaby.

Soon he is asleep, and I doze with heavy limbs aching from the day.

A twig snaps, jolting me.

Magic hangs thick in the air.

Meir's breaths even; he's still sleeping, then another crack, his body startling awake.

"What's wrong?" he asks, sleep still calling him, cupping my face.

"There's something here," I whisper. The extinguished fire has left us in darkness, then a dull light appears, radiating from Meir's hands, illuminating the forest. The light pulses with a golden glow, a beacon in the oppressive darkness. He didn't seem surprised, only alert. Shadows dance, elongated and distorted by the unnatural illumination.

Something else, something acrid, metallic overwhelms the scent of pine needles and damp earth. I think back to the trees, but I fear it is something much worse.

A guttural growl echoes from the trees, close. Meir sits alert, grabbing his sword as he gets to his feet. "Kain," he demands, his light still radiating as he scans the forest.

Lucile rising from against the tree.

He takes a step forward, the gold light intensifying, revealing a pair of luminous yellow eyes in the darkness, watching us.

"We're being surrounded," he calls to Kain, and he steps in foot beside him, sword ready for attack. I notice the fog spreading, creeping closer to our circle. No, not fog, shadows.

"Meir," I utter, my breath catching in my throat, "there's something wrong, I can feel it." My voice strains against the growing panic.

A strange sound emerges from the shadows. It sounds awful, like something near death screaming out. Something scrapes against the trees, twigs snapping as the creature moves forward, and we brace ourselves. Meir and Kain lift their swords, and we circle, looking for where the attack will come from.

The glow from Meir gives no hints of what we face; subtle sounds, and glistening eyes are swallowed by the shadows. Each pair of eyes adds to the growing number of our opponents.

That is when I see it.

The creature coming through the trees. Paws scrape the ground, breaking the tree roots as it moves, as if it is dragging its body across the forest floor. Its face looks emaciated, a starved wolf whose muscles had been removed. The fangs scraping much longer and sharper open far, unhinging its jaw. A sound that feels like nails being dragged against a blackboard.

The sound comes from the belly of the creature, a mix of screams and growls. The hairs on my arms rise, goosebumps pebbling my skin, and I feel the shiver of fear travel across my body. This creature is worse than what I saw in the dungeon all those months ago.

This creature is here for something more than just our blood. It feels as if my soul, joy, and happiness are being dragged from my chest. All aspects of my life feel like they are becoming nightmares. The creature is changing my emotions, drawing out my worst fears.

We look around and see the glint of more glowing eyes in the forest. Each creature is as horrific as the other. They move in sync, edging closer, their bodies writhing.

Meir and Kain exchanged a glance, as if they are communicating. Syncing their minds to take out the enemy. They set their stances, preparing for a battle. Their knees bent and their swords held above their shoulders.

Waiting, the creatures move closer, my body shakes with fear. "What's the plan? Does anyone have any ideas?"

I looked at Meir. Is this the end? Does it have to end this way? No.? I will not roll over and allow defeat. Lucile stands to my side, her fangs hissing.

The creatures stop. Their bodies contort, bones pop, and skin stretches. They stand on hind legs, their mouths dripping with black, rotting saliva. Their skin stretches against the bone, hair in patches and thin. Their eyes are pitch black with just the glow from Meir reflecting. They glisten.

It feels like a vortex tries to suck me in. Behind the endless dark, for the briefest instant, I swear I caught a flash of orange. It glimmers like ember sparks. Panic floods me, twisting my stomach. My ears ring as I'm brought back to the eyes in the dungeon.

My shadows surge, spilling out of my hands to wrap around the creatures, but the moment they touched them, my shadows recoiled, snapping back like snakes. The shadows do not obey me. My shadows scream in my head, curling up as if they are hurt. I call on them again, and as soon as they touch, it feels like lightning striking my entire body.

Meir's light flares brighter, the gold glow crackling against the air, illuminating every hideous fang and claw. The creatures hiss, shrinking back, not from me, but from him. His power surges as mine crumbles. Kain's sword gleams in the strange light, steady as always, the mortal anchor between us. I turn to Lucile and see her shadows recoil just as mine did.

The creatures edge closer. Their arms sag far, extending below their knees. The fingers end in yellow claws. Their teeth are razors, their tongues forking, tasting the air. The air is thick with a putrid stench. They are something unnatural. Repulsive. My stomach churns as the smell of decay grows around us.

I try one last time, shadows spilling from my skin, and again, they vanish into the blackness, feeding the enemy. I reach down for my hidden blade, my hand shaking but steady enough. If this is how it ends, it will be with steel in my grip, not the treachery of shadows. I raise my blade, and the monsters raise their claws, and their shadows flood the forest floor.

THIRTY-EIGHT
SEER

Blood drips from my mouth, a crimson tide staining the pristine white floor. The metallic tang fills my senses as I stare into the silver eyes of my tormentor. Cold. Unwavering. Relentless. He is the shadow that stalks every step, the architect of despair, the King who haunts my visions and my waking hours alike. He is the reason for my broken hear, why it mourns for a love once tender now lost, why it bleeds endlessly.

The rebellion — our fragile hope — is crumbling. I can feel it in the ache of my fractured ribs, in the slow unraveling of everything we have built. Every stolen weapon, every whispering prayer for freedom — all of it. Not enough. And now I am here. Bound. Broken. Captured.

His bright teeth twist into a predator's snarl as his thick hand clamps around my throat, crushing and deliberate. He found the three of us, the leader of the rebellion, as we met in secret. We have come so far, and now we are so close to defeat, yet now Alexander and Eliza lay dead on the wooden floor, their blood oozing down into the cracks.

I gasp for air as I try to pull his fingers from my throat. My lungs scream for air. Pain blooms like wildfire behind my eyes. Still, I glare at him. My nails bite his skin as I claw at his unyielding grip. His silver gaze glitters with cruel triumph. A sickening crack rings out, and darkness surges at the edges of my vision, threatening to consume me whole. He releases me and throws me against the wall.

"I will punish her because of you," he rasps, his breath hot against my face. Spit sprays onto my skin, mingling with the blood that already coats me. A mark of degradation I could not wipe away. His fist comes down, again and again, until the stones themselves seem to groan under the violence. His fists hitting me bring me closer to oblivion.

Even as my body shatters, my will clings to one truth: he will never have her. Not my daughter. Not Skia.

The blade at my side, the last secret I hide, finds my trembling hand. I clutch the knife's handle; its bone hilt slips in my bloody hands. I try to keep a firm grip. With the last of my strength, I draw it, silver flashing, in a single desperate arc. For a heartbeat, I think I have him. For a heartbeat, light cuts through the dark. I stab forward into his stomach.

But his grip is iron. He pulls my hand, wrestling the dagger away, and the world snaps shut around me like a coffin. His aura smothers every breath of resistance, every flicker of hope. My strike is nothing. There is no blood that drips from his skin. It did not pierce his skin. Only a tear in his robes. No wound. His skin was marble and impenetrable.

His shadows transport us from the rebel meeting place, leaving the other leaders' bodies burning in flame, to the doorway of the dungeon. He drags me down the steps, my body breaking against each cold stone, until the dungeon door slams shut like the tolling of a funeral bell. The air below is thick with rot and despair, alive with the ghosts of those who have screamed before me. Here, hope may not exist. Here, he will draw out my end.

"Summon the hounds," he growls, his voice echoing through the cavernous dark. The words are a promise, not a command. "And make sure they find her!" he yells.

Terror cuts through me sharper than any blade. Whatever fate the prophecy once promised has already shifted. My careful readings, my visions, all of them, are useless in the face of this snare he has set. The prophecy has been twisted and reshaped by his will.

But even as dread consumes me, one vow anchors me: he can destroy me, but he will never destroy her.

Skia must live.

She was an ember.

The only hope left.

The hounds howl in the dark. Their shadows take them away. Despite that, I cling to that thought. If nothing else, she must endure.

THIRTY-NINE
SKIA

The future hangs there, teasing me — how quickly things can change, and they *will* change. Something that is written can be unraveled in an instant, and I feel it slipping through my fingers.

I step forward and swing my blade.

The creature before me mocks me. Its body shakes, convulsing, and then darkness pours out of it, shadows spreading across the ground like a flood.

They swirl and twine up my legs, each slither colder than the last. They climb with a swiftness that defies their form, a viscous black tide rising against my skin. A suffocating wave of nothingness overtakes me. They coat me completely, a shroud of shadow.

At first, like a hand, they caress my face — chilling me to the core — and then violently shove themselves down my throat. They force themselves down, prying my mouth wider, and my head falls back. A silent scream rips at my vocal cords, but gurgling is all that answers. My body shakes with the force of the shadows, and tears pour from my eyes. The shadows sear my nose, blackening my eyes. They are everywhere, surrounding and suffocating.

My body rises, lifted by an unseen force. I am a puppet, strung up by the very power that should have been mine to command. I try to call on my shadows, but nothing comes. My body slams into a tree, thrown with such force that if I had any air, it would escape me.

Pain radiates through every bone. The blade is laughable now, useless and forgotten. As my body crashes onto the ground, the shadows retreat. The world tilts, a kaleidoscope of fractured light. A final, shuddering breath escapes, misting the air. Then, only the cold, consuming dark.

I lay on the ground gasping for breath, but they aren't finished. They slither back, wrapping around my throat, tightening, until the small tunnel of vision I had left fills with sparkling lights. My body grows heavy, yet I feel weightless, as if my soul is already leaving.

And then—heat.

It burns in my core, a sudden inferno. A blindingly white light sears into me, and the shadows loosen their grip. I gasp, breath tearing back into my lungs. When my eyes focus, I see them. Blue eyes, pure and radiant, search my face. Concern etches into every line.

Meir.

His hands roam urgently, searching for wounds with a desperation that matches the battle's chaos. Gentle fingers sweep tangled hair from my face as if I am something fragile and precious. I see his lips form words, feel the vibration of his concern, but the world is muffled—drowned beneath the thunder in my ears. Yet, the warmth of his presence anchors me, fighting back the numb exhaustion threatening to drag me under. My eyelids flutter, heavy with fatigue, while darkness coils at the edges of my vision, waiting to pull me back into oblivion.

Shaking.

My body is shaking.

Someone is shaking me.

With the clash of steel ringing in the background, the guttural roars of creatures echoing. All I can see are his eyes — sapphire, piercing, and pulling me into their depths. Darkness threatens to take me again. I am dizzy, my vision blurs, and my heart hammers in my chest. His face is close to mine, his calloused fingers gentle on my cheek.

Relief. Desperation. I reach up and grab his face, tangling my fingers in his golden hair, pulling his mouth to mine. Our lips meet, fire sparking, heat melting, the icy chill clinging to me. The kiss deepens — a demand, a possession, a desperate promise. This kiss is anything but a gentle touch. It is a life-altering demand. His warmth melts the walls I built for years, breaking through the frozen barricade around my heart.

The kiss shatters when the battle noise overwhelms.

"A little help here would be appreciated," Kain shouts. The sound of fighting, swords striking creatures and the creatures' growls.

I blink, and devastation stretches in every direction my gaze lands. Fallen shadow creatures are strewn across the forest floor, their forms collapsing into heaps that slowly dissolve, wisps of darkness seeping back into the earth as if the forest itself hungrily absorbs each remnant. The air reeks of charred fur and scorched soil, heavy with the metallic tang of blood and magic. Amid the ruin, Kain stands battered but unbroken—his armor dented and spattered with blood, one sleeve torn and clinging to his arm. He faces down the final hulking beast, its eyes burning with feral wrath, muscles rippling beneath thick shadowed hide. Kain's sword gleams fiercely as he moves, every motion laced with exhaustion and determination, his breaths coming in ragged bursts as he circles the creature, ready for whatever desperate charge might come next. The years of training tighten his muscles.

Meir steps forward. His shoulders tense, the muscles showing through his torn shirt. He moves forward almost as if he glides, his body etched in his glow. Light erupts from his hand. Golden, radiant, alive. It slams into the creature's chest, blooming outward in a corona that consumes it. The light pours from Meir's hands, lighting the entire forest. The trees look as if they are retreating from the sun. Then the monster crumbles, disintegrating. Its shadows and ash soak into the floor.

Lucile drops to her knees beside me and places a hand on my head. Her touch is cool against the pounding of my head. She is gentle, and I raise my hand to feel the damage. My vision is still blurred, and I can feel the pulse, the throb. My stomach is in knots. Her cool hand stays on my head as she speaks. She says the words, old familiar words, words that Ashmore would recite when he found me and Raven, hurt and in need of mending. More times than not, Raven would fetch him to mend the bruises my father left on me. A wound that was much harder to heal.

As the ache in my head lessens, I can see clearly, and the dizziness only lingers slightly. "There, you still need to rest. The wounds you had still take a toll on your body." Lucile finishes as her hand leaves my forehead and helps me to my feet.

Meir's light blankets the forest, serene and almost angelic. He meets my gaze, and his smile trembles, fierce and grateful, as if relief has cracked open in his chest. Beneath the fatigue carved into his features is a raw thankfulness, a silent, aching joy that I am safe, that after everything, the woman he loves stands before him, alive.

"Thanks for that help," Kain teases, voice low but edged with humor. "Though I *almost* had it. You could've just let me win one for once," he says to Meir.

Kain strides over, grasps his arm, and pulls him into his arms. He hugs him, murmuring gratitude. But my attention lingers on the light still clinging to Meir's skin, sparks dancing in the air. The air crackles with residual energy. I see tiny specks of light, like captured stars, still swirling around Meir's form. The warmth of the embrace and the relief in Kain's voice contrast with the lingering, electric tingle on my skin.

A question whispers in my heart, cold and sharp.

Is Meir a threat?

I have never witnessed such raw, unadulterated light power, a force capable of not only harming but ending the shadows.

And I ... I am the shadows.

The tendrils of darkness that I can usually command, the whispers that dance in my periphery, seem to shrink away, cowed by the residual energy that still crackles around Meir. He stands bathed in a golden glow that emanates from within, his face serene and almost ... ethereal. It sharply contrasts the twisted, corrupted figures I know, the creatures of darkness I deem kin. The power I wield, the ability to manipulate the shadows, is born of the same chaos and despair that birthed them. Meir's light, however, feels alien, almost holy.

Can such power understand, or worse, could it obliterate the very essence of who I am? The thought sends a chill down my spine, a primal fear that resonates deeper than any darkness I have ever known. Meir's light makes me feel vulnerable, exposed, like a moth drawn to a flame, knowing it will consume me.

Is he my salvation—or my destruction?

My shadows shiver around my ankles. And then, faint, so faint I almost think I imagined it, a voice slithers through the back of my mind.

He will be your end.

FORTY
MEIR

I see her fear blossom behind Skia's eyes, a stark contrast to the determination I have come to rely on. The flickering remnants of shadows in the clearing make her features appear sharper, more fragile, as though she might vanish if I look away. When my light ripped through the shadow creatures, she pulled back from me.

She is blameless. She has lived her whole life in the shadows. To her, light is just as terrifying as darkness is to me. In light, betrayal is a secret you cannot hide. But the thought of her being afraid of me. Afraid of *what I am*. It is unbearable.

My feelings for her have grown into something far more consuming than I ever expected. From the first moment I saw her, there had been a spark, irritating at first, then impossible to ignore. With every shared breath, every brush of her gaze against mine, that spark became a roaring fire. And after the visions Lucile has shown me ... visions of our fates intertwined in ways I could not yet understand... I knew Skia was more than I had ever dared to hope for. She is not just a companion on this path. She is the path. The missing half. The moon to my sun, casting her own light and making mine meaningful. She is an oasis in my desert, giving me life when I was certain I was lost to thirst. She is everything.

The future ahead of us is uncertain, veiled in prophecy and whispered warnings. But I know one thing with a certainty that went deeper than reason. I need her by my side. I want her as my queen, not by duty, not by alliance, but because every fiber of me has already chosen her.

There is still so much to face. The weight of our past, the looming threat of King Morthal, the perilous balance our union would tip. But the force between us — magnetic, undeniable — is no longer something I can resist. Together, I believe we can change the world. My light will not destroy her shadows. Her shadows are not the twisted abominations we fought in the forest. They are hers. Fierce, beautiful, and part of her. And if she cannot yet see their worth, I will show her.

I cross the small space between us and frame her face in my hands. Her skin is chilled, streaked with grime and blood, her braid unraveling where the battle had tugged it loose. Wisps of her hair fell over her green eyes. She is exhausted, every line of her body sagging with the toll of what she has endured. And yet, she is the most beautiful woman I have ever seen. Strong, unyielding, scarred, and alive.

Her eyes flicker up to meet mine, guarded, as if bracing for rejection. I brush her hair back, tucking the loose strands behind her ear. "You don't even see it, do you?" I whisper, though perhaps only my own soul hears the words.

Before doubt can steal her from me, I pull her close. My mouth finds hers, and the world dissolves. Her lips are soft, hesitant, then yielding as she sighs into me and draws me tighter against her. The taste of her is fire and storm, wild and impossible to contain. It ignites within me, burning right through my soul. I memorize every shift, every breath, every fleeting reaction as if this moment can be stolen from us at any second.

I kiss her as if that can convince her. As if it can carve into her the truth she refuses to see. She is not broken, not cursed, not unworthy. She is everything.

And gods help me. I will spend my life making her believe it.

FORTY-ONE
SKIA

His sudden decision startles me. His mouth presses against mine—soft, hesitant, waiting for my permission. Every part of me aches to answer. To surrender. To give in to the bond pulling us together. I long to be his, and I want him to be mine. No matter if I am the darkest of shadows and he is the brightest of lights. Together, we are the balance.

Fire and void, sun and smoke.

Every star I have ever wished on has led me here, to him. My radiant sun. The one strong enough to chase away the darkness that haunts me, the one who can take my shadows and make them disappear in light. The need is overwhelming, a tidal wave crashing over me, threatening to consume me if I do not give in.

His scent, a mix of fresh rain and warm earth, is a heady aroma that fills my senses. His hands, gentle yet firm, wrap my body, urging me closer, for his body to consume my soul. The forest around us stills, as though the trees themselves bend toward this moment, holding their breath. In his eyes, deep and unwavering blue, I see the same longing that roars inside me.

My breath catches, shallow and frantic, as warmth blooms in my core and spreads outward, tingling at my fingertips. Sweat dampens my skin, and my heart pounds, each beat a frantic drum against the silence. Blood roars in my ears, a storm echoing the desire tearing through me. Even the shadows at my feet tremble, restless, as though they too yearn for his light.

When he breaks away, it feels like severing a lifeline. My lungs burn, desperate for air. Gasping, I pull back, eyes locking onto his sky-blue gaze. The intensity still lingers, heavy between us, thick with unspoken vows and the sharp edge of fear.

Trembling, I whisper, "I do not know how, but you are mine, and I am yours. I want to complete the bond, to make it undeniable. I hunger to be yours forever. Until the sun no longer shines, until the three moons fall from the sky."

The vow carves itself from the deepest part of me. As I speak, a weight lifts from my shoulders. The suffocating terror I have carried begins to loosen, the shadows clinging to me receding like mist before dawn.

He looks at me then, and his face softens. The hard lines of his jaw ease, and he smiles. A smile that reaches his eyes, radiant, and whole, a sunrise breaking through endless twilight. A promise. A release.

"You saved me," I murmur, my voice thick with tears. "I thought I would be consumed by their shadows. But your light saved me. You pulled me back."

Meir brushes his thumb gently across my cheek, wiping away a tear. "I will always find you, no matter how deep the darkness," he whispers, his voice steady and reverent. "You are not alone. Not now, not ever. As long as my light burns, it will lead you home."

His words wrap around me, warm and sure, anchoring me in this new dawn. In his gaze, I see not just promise but certainty. An unspoken vow that whatever shadows may come, he will face them with me. My heart steadies, fear giving way to hope. For the first time, I believe the darkness might never return.

Relief and joy wash through me, sharp enough to sting my eyes. I want him to know his light does not frighten me, that it steadies me. My shadows are endless, but he saves me in more ways than I can name. For the first time, I feel peace. Safety. Wholeness. The darkness no longer holds the same power. He is my light, and I am his.

Breathless, I intertwine my hands with his. "Do you know how to complete the bond?"

Before he can answer, footsteps tread through the underbrush. Lucile emerges from the shadows. Kain follows close behind, his presence steady and reassuring, the quiet strength in his gaze grounding us both.

Lucile's eyes meet mine, warm and knowing. She kneels beside us, her hands gentle as she examines our entwined fingers. "The bond is ancient," she breathes, her voice a soothing melody in the tense hush. "Few know how to form it, but I can guide you."

Kain settles himself beside Meir, offering silent support. His hand rests on Meir's shoulder, a gesture of solidarity that bolsters the courage fluttering inside me.

"To complete the bond, you must share both your light and your darkness. It is not just pain, but surrender.

Trust each other. Let your souls intertwine." She explains each step with quiet confidence, walking us through the ritual. How to mix our blood, how to say the words that will bind us forever.

Kain, always the protector, keeps watch, his gaze never leaving us, his presence a silent promise that we are safe. Lucile's instruction steadies my nerves, her wisdom guiding us through fear and uncertainty. With their aid, we prepare to finish what we began. To become whole together, in light and in shadow.

"Are you ready?" she asks.

He nods his head, golden hair falling into his eyes. I also nod in agreement, a smile tugging at the corner of my mouth.

Fear and excitement flicker across his features as he draws the knife from his belt. Lucile goes over each step. Its silver blade shimmers in the starlight. He raises his hand, and with a swift slice, light spills from the wound—brilliant, ethereal, illuminating the shadows around us.

I take the blade from his trembling hand. Repeating the steps. My skin is clammy, my pulse racing. I draw a deep breath and slice my palm. Darkness falls from my palm, thick and viscous, pouring into the night. The smell of iron and smoke rises between us.

The shadows reach for his light, twisting, intertwining. Light and shadow dance together, merging, binding. My soul collides and intertwines with his. Our souls become one, a heart stitched together.

Our palms together, blood and bond mingling. Energy erupts, a vortex of light and shadow swirling around us, nearly shattering me. The sensation defies words. Pain and ecstasy, as though I am being torn apart and remade in the same breath.

His agony mirrors mine, etched into the lines of his face. Yet neither of us breaks away. His light burns through me, searing my veins with every pulse, while my shadows coil into him, an icy flood sinking into his core.

The bond weaves itself between us, each heartbeat a stitch pulling tighter. His skin darkens with my shadows, etched by a permanent stain. Mine glows with his light, branded with his fire. And still we hold on, our voices rising together. Words not our own spill from our lips, ancient and inevitable.

"Sha'darei vah' theil," I force the syllables past gritted teeth, the sound of the old gods tearing through me.

"Eil'mor nyra'ke," he answers, his deep voice steady, an anchor in the storm.

Light and shadow collided in one last burst, an explosion shakes the forest to its roots. The trees sway, leaves scattering like sparks in the wind. Then, with terrifying grace, the power sinks into us, merging flesh and spirit, binding us whole.

Moments pass. Silence falls. Night wraps around us like velvet, an intimate witness to the sacred vow we have forged. The three moons hang overhead—red, blue, and silver—watching like ancient sentinels, as if they too bore witness to our bond.

Kain and Lucile exchange a knowing glance. They allow us to have privacy but also want us to know they are protecting us. Lucile closes her eyes, chanting a prayer beneath her breath, her hands pressed to the earth. Kain grips his sword, ready should anything go wrong, his presence a silent promise that help stands close by.

After the attack, I feel safe. For the first time, I feel complete. Whole. Belonging. His sapphire eyes, reflecting the waters of an oasis, find mine.

"You are mine now," he whispers, voice raw. "Shadows and all. Forever. I will shield you always, and you will be my queen. You will stand by my side until the darkness takes us both."

A vow sealed in blood and breath, carved into the fabric of our souls.

And then he kisses me.

My mind, usually a battlefield of self-doubt and anxieties, struggles to comprehend the reality unfolding before me. I question my thoughts, because I feel unworthy of this, of the fierce devotion radiating from him, of the future he painted in our whispered words. This was more than love, deeper than love, a primal connection that resonates within the very core of my being. I have never felt so safe as in his arms. My world, the one I had always known, was a harsh landscape of betrayal, a desolate expanse where hate bloomed like a poisonous flower, and where the feeling of never being enough was a constant, suffocating companion.

But in his arms, the world shifts. I know what love is, truly understand its profound beauty, and how amazing it can be. I feel it deep in my soul, a certainty that pulses with every beat of my heart, that we will change the world together.

Looking into his blue eyes, eyes that hold the universe and promise eternity, I feel the world shift, my soul smiles, and I know, with a conviction that borders on divine revelation, that together, we will save our lands. The weight of my past, the darkness that had haunted my waking hours, seems to dissipate, replaced by the incandescent promise of a shared destiny.

FORTY-TWO
SKIA

None of us sleep after the attack. Every shift of the wind, every snap of a twig sends me flinching. Dawn arrives fast, and with barely enough rest to dull the edges of fear, we pack what little we carry and press forward. We have no choice.

We move deeper, and the trees grow taller, their branches knitting together into a vast canopy that swallows the sun. The forest breathes magic. It whispers from the soil, hums through the air — a current strong enough to push us forward even as our bodies beg for rest. The closer we draw to the ruins, the more the trees thin, shards of golden light slipping through the branches as though the land itself wants us to see what lies ahead.

Life stirs here. It thrives more than anything I have ever seen. Bright-eyed animals dart across our path, and birds sing from the canopy in a chorus so full it echoes through the woods. This place feels different. The magic is not heavy or suffocating but light, like a gentle breeze against my skin. A promise carries through the air. Answers. Hope.

And then the forest opens.

Emerald grass blankets the ground, glowing with an otherworldly sheen. Each thump of our horses' hooves begin to mute against the lush grass and moss that coat the path. The roar of waterfalls thunders from beyond the cliffs, their spray misting the air with silver droplets. Towering trees, ancient and wise, rise in solemn guardianship. Their trunks bear the weight of centuries, clothed in velvet moss and tangled vines. Amid them stand the remnants of a forgotten world—stone arches and broken walls, half-claimed by ivy. Birds nest in the crevices, their songs weaving life back into ruins long abandoned.

It is breathtaking, a tapestry of history and wild magic. With each step, my shadows loosen, they feel free here. The exhaustion I had worn like armor melts away, replaced by something dangerously close to peace. Even Meir's smile seems brighter here, his shoulders unburdened, his body loosening as though the air itself coaxes the tension from his frame.

Lucile still weaves in and out with her shadows, though her strides seem lighter. Kain rides beside us, in awe of the forest that we've entered.

"This place is astonishing," he says looking around at each plant and animal that surrounds us.

"Everything I see is perfect," Meir says, though his gaze doesn't leave my body. I can feel his eyes burning into me.

"You're not even seeing it Meir! You're just staring at Skia," Kain answers. "Of course I mean no offense my Queen." he says winking.

Meir clears his throat. His lips brush the curve of my neck, his fingers slipping into my hair. Every touch sends shivers through me, but not the kind born of fear. They are reminders that happiness—strange, untainted happiness—is possible.

"Do you think we'll reach the ruins before nightfall?" I ask, leaning back into him. I didn't want the answer. Reaching the end meant leaving this sanctuary, returning to his kingdom, and sparking a war I dreaded. My father will never approve of me being the Queen of the Light

Lands. Every lie he spoke was unfolding right before my eyes. I want to linger in this in-between, where nothing yet demands blood, where the world feels untouched.

Meir's mouth curves against my ear. "What thoughts play in that mind of yours? Your face is a book—beautiful, waiting to be read. I've only glimpsed the first pages, yet I already know it's a story I'll never tire of."

His words unravel me. Ahead, Kain and Lucile travel close, laughter and quiet words passing between them. I catch the spark there and let myself imagine—just for a heartbeat—a world where our two realms might be united not through conquest, but through bonds like these.

"I am nothing but shadows," I confess, the words slipping free before I can stop them. "I am darkness. Unworthy of you. My shadows will smother your light."

I feel his body respond, his worry tightening his touch. His voice comes low, steady, a vow made for me alone. "You may carry shadows, but you are not made of them. I am yours, wholly and forever. Your darkness does not diminish me, Skia. It makes my light shine brighter. Without it, there would be nothing to illuminate. You are everything I have ever needed. Your past cannot change that. Whatever shadows follow you, I will meet them with my light."

His fingers trace a final line across my cheek, burning away the last of the fear. His words sink deeper than any blade, cutting through doubt until all that remains is truth.

In that moment, I let the bond settle inside me, quieting every whisper that tells me I am less. He is mine. I am his. Forever.

FORTY-THREE
MEIR

The path has changed so much in only a few hours. This land feels untouched, as though no mortal has stepped here in centuries. The air is thick with the fragrance of blossoms I do not know, sweet and herbal, clinging to the damp earth. Above us, the sky swirls with charcoal-gray clouds. It is cool, a slight breeze twisting through my hair.

The very air hums with a quiet energy. This place feels like neither kingdom. Untouched by war, a neutral zone holding its own forgotten truths. I wonder what my father has never told me. His stories of gods have always been simple. Mortals lived in purity and light. Shadows belonged in darkness. Black and white. But this land whispers of shades between.

The silence presses around us, full of secrets waiting to be unearthed. By nightfall, our muscles ache from the endless journey. The tension of every mile has carved lines into us all.

"Lucile," I rasp, my voice dry from dust and worry, "how much farther? The Seer's vision, where does it lead us?" We are gathered around the fire. The soft grass beneath wraps around my fingers as I lean back on my hands. Skia lays beside me, her head on my lap, looking up to the stars above.

Lucile glances at me, her ruby eyes glinting. "We are close. This is where the gods once walked. They shaped the world here. Some saw strength in uniting light and dark, while others feared it. The goddess—she believed the two belonged together. She gave mortals both, creating balance. But fear prevailed. Hunters were born to chase down any who sought to challenge the gods' decree. Now they hunt Skia."

Her words cut through me like a blade. Skia's eyes look to mine as I search her face. Her perfect green eyes are the same color of the grass that we gather on. The thought of losing Skia, of someone tearing her from me, is unbearable. If they take her, I will burn this world down to ash to get her back.

Lucile's voice drops lower. "This land thrived once, filled with beings of immense power. But ambition destroyed them. They forced the goddess into a union she did not want, and in their arrogance, they unraveled everything."

Her words linger like smoke, fragments of a broken story we will have to piece together ourselves. "What union?" I ask.

"A mortal," she says, leaving out any information. It drives me insane at times, when she is so vague while also being all knowing. Knowledge is a weapon, and Skia and I will need it if we are to survive what is coming.

The air thickens with tension. Kain's voice snaps like a whip. "Why have we never heard of this goddess?"

Lucile laughs soft, unsettling. "How do you know you haven't?"

Shadows flicker against the temple walls where we rest, grotesque carvings twisting in the torchlight. For a moment, her gaze catches mine, and I feel it, a kinship, an understanding of truths buried beneath everything we think we know.

The silence that follows screams louder than any warning.

FORTY-FOUR
MEIR

That night, frustration claws at me like a living thing. Every choice I make presses heavier than armor. My kingdom waits—my people wait—and I have in a way abandoned them. What if my absence has already doomed them? What if enemies stand at the gates while their king sleeps in foreign ruins, chasing shadows of prophecy?

The faces of my people haunt me. Farmers who trust me to guard their fields, soldiers who have sworn their lives to my banner, children who have been raised to believe the light will always protect them. I have left them with uncertainty, and the weight of that betrayal sinks deep into my chest.

My father's voice whispers from memory, sharp and unyielding: *"A king's first duty is to his people. Everything else is a weakness."*

Am I weak, then? Have I traded my kingdom for the girl beside me? Or have I finally broken free of his narrow vision of the world?

I turn to Skia, and the answer softens inside me. She is the piece I didn't know was missing, the one thing that makes sense in the chaos. Before her, my life had been a script written in black and white, duty and obedience carved into me by my father's hand. With her, the world is no longer gray, it bleeds with color. And fragile though it is, there is hope.

The forest around us breathes differently than anywhere else I have been. Chirps and rustles, the prowl of unseen creatures, the rushing of waterfalls—it pulses with life. A breeze stirs through the grass, carrying the perfume of wildflowers. It is a stark contrast to the Geheimnis Forest we have crossed, where silence presses down like a curse and every breath felt stolen. That place drained us, testing us, pushing us to the edge. Here, it feels as though the land itself offers us rest, as if the ruins themselves want us to remember the gods have been lost.

I stretch out beside Skia and press a kiss to her cheek, then pull her into my arms. Her hair smells impossibly sweet—vanilla and sugared plums, a fragrance that defied the road. Many days of dirt, of sweat, of restless nights, and still she smells of life. She hasn't complained once, but I see it. The storm gathering behind her eyes. Determination tempered with worry.

She is magic in motion. Watching her is like standing before a sunrise, you are seeing for the first time. Brilliant, dangerous, impossible to look away from. She is strength where I falter, the reminder that love can burn hotter than fear.

The ruins glow faintly in the moonlight. Vines climb the broken arches, their leaves silvered by starlight. The three moons hang above us, silver, blue, and red, each one watching like a sentinel. Their light draped across Skia's skin, painting her in hues both ethereal and mortal.

Skia is quiet as I thread my hand through her hair. Kain and Lucile lie near us. We all lay on the soft ground. There is a tranquility to this place, something that settles in my soul.

My father had always spoken of the gods as unbending rulers who had divided the world in their wisdom, light to one side, shadow to the other. But Lucile's words still ring in my mind. What if he had been wrong? What if the gods had wanted unity, and men like my father twisted their stories into weapons of control?

The thought terrifies me. If the gods themselves had once believed in balance, then all our wars, all our bloodshed, have been for nothing. Entire generations lost to a lie.

I stare up at the moons and wonder how much of my life has been built on falsehoods. "Does anyone else feel a strange energy? Like inner peace since we arrived here?" I ask.

Kain shifts on the grass, propping himself up on one elbow. The glow of the moons catches in his eyes as he considers my question. "It's... different here," he admits, his voice quieter than usual, threaded with a reverence I rarely hear from him. "When I was a boy, my grandmother told stories of the old gods—how they'd walk among us in places like this, where the veil between our world and theirs was thin. She said you could feel them if you listened close enough."

Lucile lets out a soft laugh, though her gaze is fixed on the ruins. "Your grandmother was wise, Kain. My mother used to say that too. But she warned me that the peace in places like this isn't always kindness—it's memory. The gods left their echoes behind, and sometimes those echoes want to be heard."

I glance between them, curiosity blossoming. "Do you think that's what we're feeling? The old gods, or what's left of them?"

Kain nods, running a hand through his hair. "Maybe. Or maybe it's hope. They say the gods divided the world, but what if all those lines—light and dark, truth and lies—are just stories we tell ourselves? Maybe the gods wanted something simpler. Balance. Unity."

Lucile's eyes glimmer in the moonlight, thoughtful. "If that's true, it would mean everything we've been taught—about war, about who deserves the light—could be wrong. Maybe the gods weren't rulers at all. Maybe they were guardians. And maybe stories like ours are how their memory survives."

Silence settles, but it's not uncomfortable. In the hush, I realize how little we truly know—and how much more there is to learn about the history we've inherited, and the gods we've lost.

Skia squeezes my hand. "We're not alone in the world, even when it feels like it. Maybe the gods are gone, or maybe they're waiting for us to remember what unity feels like."

I nod, feeling the peace of the ruins settle deeper in my chest, the conversation weaving together threads of old stories and newfound hope.

I tighten my hold on Skia, unwilling to let even the night steal her warmth. My doubts, my fears, my father's voice. They all recede when I breathe her in. She is the only constant in a world unraveling, the anchor in the storm of duty and prophecy.

Her fingers graze mine, light but sure, and in that touch is everything I need. I turn to her, the words flooding past my mouth before I can stop them—quiet, reverent, carrying all the weight of my heart. "You do not know how much you mean to me, Skia," I whisper. "You're my peace in all this chaos. When I look at you, the world makes sense again. I can't wait for the day when you're truly by my side—not just as my anchor, but as my queen."

My thumb traces gentle circles across her knuckles. "I want everyone to know it. I want the world to see what I see—to understand that you're my light, my hope, the reason I keep going. Whatever comes, whatever the old stories demand of us, I promise I'll be there. I'll fight for you, for us. And when the time comes, I'll be proud to stand beside you, as your king, and call you my queen, no matter what else we may face."

Whatever awaits us, gods, Hunters, war. I know one truth with absolute certainty. She is mine. And I will not let her go.

FORTY-FIVE
MEIR

We wake, and the sun shines bright along the lush forest floor. Highlighting every vine, tree, and stone. The day is long, heavy with travel. It feels as if all travel is uphill. The horses' hooves propel us and slide on the wet ground as storms build around us.

The air hangs humid, and sweat clings to our skin. A hush settles over the forest, broken only by the distant rumble of thunder—a sound so unfamiliar it feels almost sacred. Storms are rare in the Light Lands. Each one is a marvel, a reminder of the world's wildness. I lift my gaze as the clouds gather, swirling in shifting layers of gray and violet, their darkness deepening with every heartbeat. The light dims, a hush falling over bird and beast alike, as if the whole land waits, breath held, for what comes next.

Another roll of thunder shakes the land. The horses seem unaffected by it, nearer now, its echo lingering long after. The wind stirs, sharp and electric, carrying the scent of rain and distant lightning. Cool drops patter down—first one, then many—streaking our faces, soaking our clothes, and dappling the earth in widening circles. I watch as the raindrops weave glistening threads across Skia's skin, see the way each leaf bends beneath their weight, and marvel at how the world transforms under the storm's touch. I am in awe—the power, the beauty, the rare violence of the sky reminding me how small we are. Every sense is heightened, every detail sharper, as if the storm is washing the world clean and letting us begin again.

Skia laughs when the first drops kiss her cheek, and the sound is bright and crystalline, cutting through the heavy air like sunlight through a storm cloud. Her joy echoes through the trees, so infectious that even Kain can't help but smile. Around us, the forest feels different. Older, stranger, humming with a power deeper than the storm itself. The air tingles against my skin, charged with something ancient, and the hairs on my arms stand on end.

Towering trees arch overhead, their gnarled trunks and tangled branches sheltering shifting pockets of shadow and sudden bursts of light as the wind moves through the canopy.

I lean forward in the saddle, Skia's back warm and solid against my chest while rain runs down our faces, cold but somehow invigorating. I glance at Kain riding just beside us, his cloak plastered to his shoulders, and call out over the rain, "Feels like magic, doesn't it?"

Kain tips his head back, eyes closed as droplets bead and slide down his nose. "It's incredible," he says with a broad grin. "The rain—like the gods themselves are blessing us. I'd almost forgotten what thunder sounded like."

Lucile drifts at the edge of my vision, slipping between tree trunks and ducking under broad leaves to escape the heaviest downpour. She moves with uncanny grace, vanishing and reappearing, her cloak swirling behind her. Now and then, she pokes her head out, flashes a mischievous smile, then disappears again just as another gust sends sheets of rain through the clearing.

Skia tips her face up to the sky, laughing again, her eyes bright with delight. "Let her hide—some of us prefer to embrace the storm," she says, pressing closer against me. I wrap my arm tighter around her waist, feeling the rain soak us both, joining us to this wild, sacred place.

Kain's horse steps into a puddle, splashing water up his boots, and he shakes his drenched hair out of his eyes. "We're lucky," he says more quietly now, "lucky to see the world like this. Lucky we're together."

The rain thickens, the steady rhythm pounding the leaves as the storm renews its power. For just a moment, everything else fades. The gods' presence, the threat of prophecy, the old stories waiting for us. There's only the rain, our laughter, and the raw, electric joy of being alive under a sky that feels crafted just for us.

We stop near a stream to rest, scavenging what little we have left for a meager meal. The crystalline water, a shimmering, sunlit ribbon, rushes over smooth, cool, gray stones, its gurgling song echoing, captivating. After days of gritty dust and grime, the cool promise of a bath is too tempting to resist.

Leaving Kain and Lucile behind, I follow Skia to the bank. Sunlight dappled, dripped through the canopy, catching my eye. It paints her in shifting gold and shadow as she sheds her worn clothes. The air held the scent of damp earth and unseen blooms. Each movement is graceful, deliberate, a hush falling as if the forest watched in reverence. Looking back at me, two green emeralds, she removes each article of clothing while maintaining eye contact. Every curve of her body makes my eyes trail along, following her hands. She enters the river. The water creeps up her body like hands.

I strip, then chase after her. The river's surface gleams, reflecting the sky. A shiver runs down my spine as the cool water bites, erasing the day's weariness. Skia submerges ahead of me, her dark hair swirling like silk beneath the surface. She rises in front of me, droplets sliding down her neck, tracing paths across her chest before disappearing into the stream.

She is a vision—part goddess, part storm. My pulse pounds with primal urgency. Her green eyes lock onto mine, reflecting both curiosity and hunger. She bites her lower lip, then closes the distance, her body brushing mine. Fingers tangle in my hair as her lips find mine.

Her kiss, a searing flame, brands my lips. Her touch, tracing each ridge and hollow, raises goosebumps on my skin. "I want you," she whispers, the words a hot breath against my mouth, stealing the very air I need.

I growl, hands grip her hips, pulling her against me as the water churns around us. My hands guide her legs around my waist, and I slide my hands up her thighs, grabbing her firm backside. Her skin is soft and inviting. For a moment, the world narrows to heat and water and the desperate ache of wanting.

A scream shatters it.

We break apart, gasping, the taste of her still on my lips. A scream, close and raw, slices the humid air. My heart hammers, a frantic drum against the echo of her kiss and the chilling dread of the sound. Skia's eyes widen, searching my face for answers.

"Did you hear that? Was that Lucile?" Her voice trembles, barely more than a whisper. I nodded, adrenaline surging. The moment shattered. Briefly, I kiss her again, a final, desperate touch.

"Later," I breathe, the promise hanging between us. She grabs my wrist, her grip urgent.

"Be careful," she says, her voice fierce despite the quiver. Cold water clings to my skin as I stumble out, my fingers clumsy with my clothing, and sprint toward camp, fear tightening in my chest. The world narrowing to the frantic need to reach them before whatever darkness comes can claim us all.

Our small camp is in chaos as I run up. I see a cloaked figure, his back turned away from me. He doesn't see or hear me, my feet falling gently on the soft ground. I see Lucile to the side. Her teeth are bared as she hisses at the man who is pinning Kain to a tree, a knife at his throat. Lucile is kneeling on the ground, shadow ropes spinning around her containing her.

"Are you going to do something?" she mouths, trying to keep the beast's attention only on Kain.

Kain fights against the hooded figure, his hands trying to pry the pale hand from his throat. The assailant uses all its strength to keep Kain flat against the tree. He speaks, his voice low and inhuman.

"Where is she?" he demands. "I can *feel* her shadows. Tell me where she is, boy."

The words ice my blood. Skia.

"Get off me," Kain spits in the face of the hooded figure.

He doesn't flinch as Kain spits, his grip tightens. "Where is she?" the figure growls again. The pale hand, almost bone-like, is a wisp of shadows made whole. Its edges flowing up and down, lashing out, slithering tongues toward Kain.

I scan the camp, eyes locking on my sword. It is lying just behind the figure. Adrenaline surges through my body, mapping out every step I need to take to get to it. I bolt, sliding across the grass, I reach my hand toward my sword, closing around the hilt. I roll onto my knees and spring toward the beast. Swinging with all my strength, I connect with the blade. Yet instead of cleaving flesh, the figure dissolves into a torrent of shadows, scattering like smoke. My strike cuts air, the edge grazing the tip of Kain's nose. He falls, coughing, crimson dripping onto the dirt.

The shadows fall from Lucile. Her eyes snap to Kain. I see a moment of hesitation as she watches the blood dripping from Kain's nose.

"Close enough Meir!" he yells, holding his nose, blood covering his hand.

Lucile walks over, muttering as she reaches for Kain's face. Healing as magic flows from her. The blood that dripping from his nose slows, as the wound closes. "Magic is nice," he says with a grin on his face.

"Magic is wonderful," I say, managing a weak smile.

Soft footsteps approach from behind. I turn to see Skia emerge from the shadows, her face drawn and pale, fear etched deep in her eyes.

"What happened?" she whispers, her voice trembling.

I glance at Kain, who is still gasping for breath. "That's a great question," I say, trying to steady my own nerves. "Kain, can you explain what just happened?"

Kain wipes at the blood on his face, shaking his head. His eyes are wide, still full of shock. "I don't know," he admits, his voice rough. "He was just there suddenly. He kept asking about her. Said little else. Then," he puts his hand around his throat, "shadows at my throat. "You nearly take my head off with your sword." His glare is weak but determined, tinged with a strained attempt at humor.

"You survived, didn't you?" I mutter.

Lucile stands silently by. Her hands show marks from the shadows, the bruises blooming on her tawny skin. The look in her eyes says more than words could; she knows something she isn't ready to share.

"We need to move," I say at last, my voice hoarse. "Before that thing comes back—or brings others with it."

We pack in hurried silence, the tension so thick that even the sound of rustling leaves feels like a threat. None of us speaks about what just happened, but the truth hangs heavy between us: this is no random attack. The shadows have found us. And I know they will not stop until they find her.

FORTY-SIX
MEIR

The jungle thickens until the vines knit themselves into an impenetrable wall, their green lengths so densely entwined that they consume bark, stone, and even the very air between them. I watch as the barrier pulses—slow, steady—like the living throb of a buried heart. Every inch seems alive beneath a sheath of foliage, breathing in rhythm with some hidden force. Shadows flicker and slide over the surface, hinting at movement deeper within, as if the jungle itself is aware of our approach, guarding whatever lies beyond with silent vigilance.

"Do you feel that?" Skia whispers, awe braided with apprehension.

I nod. With the pull gathering behind my ribs, a tide drawing me forward. "This way," I call to Kain and Lucile over the rising thrum.

I swing down from the saddle. The ground shifts under my boots, damp and unsteady, as if something beneath us turns in its sleep. I catch Skia's hand to help her dismount. She moves as if entranced, palm lifting toward the green curtain. The moment her fingers brush the vines, the jungle answers.

The earth trembles.

Stone groans, vibrating through the soles of my boots. Tree trunks snap with sharp, splintering cracks—spears hurled by the furious earth itself. Our horses scream in wild terror, their eyes wide and rolling as they bolt, hooves striking sparks from the rocks as they vanish down the tangled path we carved to reach this place. The ground pitches and rolls beneath us, waves of upheaval threatening to throw me off my feet. I fight my way through the chaos, reaching Skia just as she stumbles. Wrapping her tightly against my chest, I press one hand over her head, shielding us both as the world seems to tear itself loose around us, every heartbeat pounding in time with the trembling earth. I can feel her breath hitch, her body tense, and together we brace against the storm, waiting for the jungle's fury to pass—or for it to reveal what lies beneath its wrath.

Silence, as sudden as a held breath.

The vine wall shudders and falls in a single sweeping collapse, an emerald avalanche that reveals a hidden expanse beyond. Cool air, old as bones, pours over us.

Statues tower ahead—marble giants cut with impossible precision, standing in a crescent open to a roof of tangled boughs. Shadows pool at their feet, not wild but watchful, swirling in slow eddies like smoke caught in a windless room.

We step through.

Kain edges closer, jaw tight. "Your father never mentioned this." His voice sounded small beneath the weight of stone. The gods and goddesses tower in large marble statues. Each one made in perfection, their chiseled faces so perfect they look lifelike.

Lucile's eyes glitter with recognition or fear. I can't tell which. "He wouldn't," she murmurs. "The old stories were changed. Cleaned."

Skia's shadows stir against the floor like ink testing the edges of parchment, then draw back, subdued. Her fingers find mine and squeeze once, steadying me, or herself, perhaps both.

At the back of the crescent stands a goddess unlike the rest. She radiates magic, almost lifelike in the stones. Blonde curls framed a face carved with such living truth I almost say her name before I know it. Light pulses from her chest, a beacon heartbeat—thrum, thrum—that syncs with the rhythm inside my own.

Recognition hits clean and merciless.

It is my mother. Memories from my childhood flash behind my eyes.

My breath breaks. "Mother?" The word went nowhere in that stone-bright air.

Skia's hand settles on my back. I turn half toward her. Her eyes are wide, searching, full of questions I cannot answer. Why is my mother's face set among gods?

The light swells within the statute.

It spills forth and finds me like water finds its riverbed. Heat licks across my skin, then through it, a current racing in my veins. My own light surges to meet it, answering as if it has been waiting its whole life to be called. Shadows around the pedestals hiss and recoil. My knees give and I land on the stone floor, the impact lost to the burning in my chest. A scream rises that never makes it out of my throat—the sound swallows the roar inside my bones.

It is not a fire that burns flesh. It is a making, and an unmaking. Like being hammered and poured back into a mold I did not know is mine.

Somewhere far away, Kain shouts my name. Lucile is chanting words I do not know. I am lost, feeling as if I am being pulled farther away. Skia presses against me, trying to drag me away from the flood of light and failing because where can she take me? It is inside me now. Everything goes black and I cannot see the land, or Skia beside me. Cool darkness surrounds me.

A soft light appears in the darkness, moving toward me.

Not the statue—*her*. The woman from my dreams. The mother who chased me through sunlit halls, whose laughter filled rooms I thought too big to hold anything but echo. Golden hair, eyes alight with a joy made sharp by sorrow. Her feet glide toward me. She reaches and cups my cheek, and the light gentles where her hand touches, as if even power remembers to be kind for her.

"Meir," she says, and my name is a melody I had almost forgotten.

"I have little time," she continues, urgency threading her voice. "They will feel this. They will come."

"Who? Who will come?" The words scrape out raw. A thousand questions crowd my tongue.

"Listen." Her gaze holds mine, steady as anchor-stone. "The gods were divided. Some feared what they could not control. They tore the balance in two, then told mortals a story to make the tearing feel holy." Her eyes softened. "A few of us hid what we could. We seeded it where it might survive."

"Skia," I breathe, understanding breaking like dawn. "The Hunters—"

"They hunt what remembers," she says. "They hunt what makes the lie unravel."

She leans closer, voice dropping to a thread that tugs me back from the pain.

"You are half-god, Meir. Not by accident. You were born of a choice that cost everything." Grief flickered across her face and was gone. "Your light is meant to heal the rift, to mend what was broken. But light alone cannot do it. You will blind what you wish to save." Her eyes slide beyond me, to the shadow that lived in Skia like a second pulse. "You need her. Two halves of one design."

The words dug into the places the light had remade. A key turning.

"How?" I force out. "How do we fix it?"

"A betrayal will change the tides, light will return and the skies will darken,

Her gaze grows distant, as if searching the shape of things yet to come. The warmth in her touch lingers, anchoring me against the gathering darkness.

"When the betrayal comes, you must remember wounds do not close with light alone. To mend the rift, you and Skia must walk where neither wishes to go. You must descend—into the heart of what was lost, into the memory none dare hold. There, together, you will find the seed of what was divided. Only when shadow and light speak together will the world begin to heal."

Her voice trembled—not from fear, but from hope and sorrow intertwined. "Trust Skia, and let her trust you. There will be a choice that feels impossible. Choose not for yourself, but for all who carry the weight of the story. Only then will the balance return."

With each word, the soft light seemed to pulse in rhythm with my heart, steadying me, urging me to listen, to remember.

"You are not alone, Meir. Even in the darkness, goodness remains—woven in every act of mercy, in every hand offered, even when hope seems lost. That is where you will find me again."

I shake my head, breath ragged. "Why didn't you tell me? Why—"

"Because men like your father would have burned you to ash to keep the story pure," she says, not unkindly. "Because I loved you more than I feared them."

The brilliance falters. Her outline flickers—once, twice. She glances past me again. I feel rather than see Skia, close enough for her shadow to brush the edge of my vision, close enough that my light did not recoil.

"I am proud of you," my mother whispers, voice breaking on pride and some deeper wound I would never name. "You will be a different kind of king."

"Don't go," I beg, a child again.

"I never did." Her smile is small and terrible and perfect. She leans forward and presses her forehead to mine, and something burns there—a sigil drawn in light, sharp and gone before I can understand it.

The statue's glow gutted. The flood retreats, leaving a ringing emptiness in its wake. My strength went with it. I fall. My body crushing into the stone ground and all my breath leaves my body.

"Meir!"

Skia's voice cracks the air. Hands catch my shoulders; her shadows flare wild and panicked, reaching for me, for anything. Somewhere to my right, Lucile hissed a warning I could not parse—about wards waking, about shadows stirring where they had been still.

Fatigue unlike anything I have ever felt crashes into me. Holding my eyes open is impossible.

The last thing I feel is Skia's fingers at my face, and the echo of my mother's command—*choose mercy*—ringing like a bell in the hollow place the light has left behind.

Darkness closes in.

The last thing I hear is Skia's voice, raw with panic, calling my name.

FORTY-SEVEN
SKIA

I drop to my knees beside Meir, boots crunching on the cold cobblestones. His name rips from my throat, echoing through the cavernous chamber. I shake him, desperate for a twitch, a breath, a heartbeat stronger than the fragile flutter beneath my palm.

"Please…" My voice cracks, the word breaking me open. "Please wake up."

The air hums with power, sharp as lightning on the skin. Every god-statue loom above, marble faces caught between divinity and menace. Their shadows stretch, pulsing as if listening.

Kain moves behind me, slow, reverent. He reaches for the statue's face—the goddess with the golden hair—and recoils in the cold. His stoicism falters, leaving only paleness and fear.

"This is his mother," he whispers, the words barely audible.

I snapped my head toward him. "What?" The world tilts, my mind unable to grasp the truth. His *mother*? A goddess carved in stone among the ancients. How could he not have known? Or had he known all along?

Lucile's crimson eyes dart between the cold marble of the statue and Meir's still form. Silence hangs heavy, a palpable thing, thick with the metallic tang of blood. A tremor of uncertainty, perhaps fear, flickers across her face, the air charged with unspoken emotion.

"I don't understand!" My scream cracking against the marble walls, shaking loose echoes that mocked me. "He should have told me! We should have known!"

But Meir lies still, lips parted as though caught in dream, serene in a way that feels wrong. My hands trembled against his cheek, cold skin meeting the warmth of my tears. The calm on his face is unbearable when mine is unraveling.

Kain crouches beside me, voice barely more than a whisper. "Skia, he may not have known. None of us did. You're not alone in this."

I shake my head. "How could he not? How could any of us be so blind?" My voice breaks, threading through the hush. I glance at Lucile, searching for answers in her guarded eyes.

Lucile looks away, jaw set. "The gods keep their secrets well," she murmurs. "Sometimes even from their own children."

The silence presses in, filled only with Meir's fragile breathing and the electric tension in the chamber. I stroke his hair, desperate for him to stir.

"Meir, please," I whisper fiercely.

The statues hang above, ancient eyes seeming to watch, waiting for what I cannot give.

Time stretches. His head rests in my lap, his weight anchoring me in a place that feels unreal. Damp air carries the scent of stone and rain, but I barely breathe.

The shadows stir within me. A feeling of losing control takes over.

At first, they pooled gently around me, curling like smoke across the floor. Then they thicken, viscous, hungry. They pour from my skin as though my body can no longer contain them, black tendrils unfurling with a will of their own.

He will betray you, they whisper, voices layered atop one another, slithering into my mind. *He will leave you. You are only the vessel. The gods chose him, not you.*

"No." I press my forehead to Meir's, clutching his face in shaking hands. "No, that's not true."

He carries the light. You are nothing but shadow. He will cast you aside when the choice comes.

The words sink sharply into me, poison winding through my veins. Tears blur my sight, and still the whispers press in, louder, faster, drowning out thought.

Kain draws his blade, voice hard. "She's losing control."

Lucile steps between us, arms out. "Put it away. If you strike her, we all die. Can't you feel it? My Gods, Kain!"

The chamber itself is trembling now, shadows at the statues' bases writhing in sympathy with mine. Cracks splinter through marble. One god's eyes glowed faintly, watching.

I pull Meir close, cradling him tightly in my arms as his limp weight presses against my chest. Desperation claws at my throat, and I rock him back and forth, willing myself to remember the warmth of him—the only thing anchoring me against the rising tide of panic and magic in the air. Marble dust sifts down from the cracked ceiling with every tremor, and the chamber shakes with a violence that feels ready to crack the world apart. The shadows writhing at the feet of the statues mirror my own, swirling and twisting as if drawn by some dark current.

Through choking sobs, I beg, "Come back to me. Please, Meir, don't let me be lost. Don't let me drown in this madness." My voice echoes off the ancient stone, haunted and fragile.

Everything seems to pause—time hangs in suspense. Meir's lips part, and with a trembling whisper, he breathes a single word. "Mercy."

The chaos in the chamber ebbs. The air stills. The tremors cease. My shadows, which have been moving like panicked birds, freeze mid-motion and then melt away, settling into silence. The statues no longer threatens overhead, their cracked faces no longer watching, as if something unseen has calmed even the gods themselves.

I inhale sharply, my heart pounding so fiercely it feels as if it might burst. Meir's eyes are still closed, yet I feel a faint twitch in his fingers where they cling to mine—a small sign of life amid the suffocating gloom that has threatened to swallow us both.

For the first time since the blinding light from the statue engulfed him, hope pierces through the darkness surrounding us. It was fragile, but it is real—a spark that defies extinction.

FORTY-EIGHT
MEIR

The light swirls around me, a kaleidoscope of color bending the air until I can't tell up from down. My stomach lurches; panic presses sharp against my ribs. I am not where I am supposed to be.

"Skia?" My voice breaks into the blur, desperate for the tether of her presence. But the bond is faint, dull, a hollow ache where she should have been. Terror blooms.

"You are not of this world," a voice thunders from behind me, reverberating through my bones. "And yet you are not of theirs."

I spin, my breath catching in my chest, every sense on high alert. Before me stands a figure both dazzling and terrifying—radiant in a way that is almost painful to behold. He is shaped like a man, but no mortal could ever look like this. Every inch of him glows with an otherworldly brilliance: his form is sculpted from pure, gleaming gold that seems to pulse with its own internal light. His hair shimmers, each strand like sunlight forged into solid threads, cascading over his shoulders in a halo of incandescence. His skin flows like molten metal, shifting and swirling with every subtle movement, as if he is fire given human shape.

Most striking are his eyes—twin pools of living flame, swirling and deep, burning with ancient power and unknowable purpose. The heat of his gaze scorches the air between us; I feel exposed, as if every secret and every fear within me is illuminated by his relentless scrutiny. He is breathtakingly beautiful, but the beauty is edged with danger, creation entwined with annihilation—divine artistry paired with the threat of instant destruction. I am caught in the paradox: compelled to look, but desperate to turn away, awestruck and afraid all at once.

My throat tightens, words damming up behind the pressure of awe and terror. Questions—dozens, hundreds—race through my mind, demanding answers, but my tongue is useless, frozen by the magnitude of the presence standing before me. All I can do is stare, heart pounding, as the embodiment of divinity and devastation waits in silence.

He laughs—a deep, resonant sound that seems to rumble up from the earth itself, vibrating through my bones. "Always overflowing with words," he says, voice rich with amusement, "yet never truly listening. The fact that you were chosen—well, that is astonishing indeed."

Chosen. The word struck me like a blade, sharp and undeniable. A god. This is no ordinary man, no wild dream conjured by my mind.

"Why me?" The question burst out, raw and unpolished, scraping at my throat. "What am I?"

His golden eyes catch mine with searing intensity, and at once, the air thickens—soundless, breathless. In that suspended moment, everything else fades.

"When the world first came to be," he began, his tone dropping into something ancient and echoing, "we rose from the First Flame. Six gods, six keepers of balance. Lucifis, Niaxias, Nikioals, Vesselus, Illiraya, Kredoases." As he speaks each name, the space around us seems to bend and shimmer. The world blurs, and blazing images spring to life. Seven radiant figures standing over a new-born world, magic pouring from their hands, spilling into oceans and scattering stars across the sky.

"For centuries, we ruled," he continues, leaning against a wall that isn't there, his voice reverberating with both pride and arrogance. "Mortals thrived. Balance was kept. Peace endured. But then—one of us chose a mortal. That single decision shattered everything. Divine gifts were given. Powers were shared. And soon, mortals turned those gifts against each other. War erupted. Shadows were born—not as a curse, but as a crucible. Niaxias understood. Shadow is not our enemy, but a source of strength. She wanted to protect the mortals."

His golden eyes blaze with fierce conviction. His voice grows sharp, almost accusing. "But I, Lucifis, saw the truth. Shadows are weakness. They are corruption, a disease to be eradicated. And so, war followed—gods clashing with gods, mortals fighting mortals. The sun itself cracked. The land split in two. Light Kingdom. Shadow Kingdom. A wound carved deep into eternity, never to truly heal."

The images exploded, turning into a heap of ash and dancing flames. My chest heaved, a chill spreading through my unconscious body.

Lucifis's lips curl. He walks toward me, his glowing body leaving trails of gold behind. "And yet, through ruin, prophecy endures. A son of light, born to end the curse. A daughter of shadow, to rise in vengeance. Together, they would either mend the world ... or destroy it utterly."

For an instant, the weight of his words hangs in the air—heavy, crackling, impossible to ignore. My mind churns, pieces of half-remembered legends and cryptic warnings falling into place. Lucifis's gaze pins me, the golden glow of his presence illuminating truths I try to deny. It all makes sense now. The strange dreams, the power thrumming beneath my skin, the ever-present pull between light and shadow. I was the son of light, and Skia—the one I loved, the one I feared—is the daughter of shadow.

The prophecy isn't myth. It is our lives, our choices, our burden to bear. Lucifis hadn't come to threaten; he'd come to challenge, to force me to see what has been written before I ever drew breath. My pulse hammers as realization strikes—this isn't about fate, but about what we will choose. Mend the world or destroy it. The prophecy isn't a cage. It is a crossroads.

I look up, meeting Lucifis's blazing eyes. The future shimmers between us, fragile and terrible, waiting for our next step.

The light dims until only his golden face looms, close, too close. His breath sears my skin.

"Your mate will betray you," he whispers, venom wrapped in silk. His golden face is too close, leaving me feeling uneasy. "Shadows cannot be trusted. They will consume you, and she will turn against you when it matters most."

His hand rises, fingers gleaming like a blade. The air presses heavy on my chest. My heart thunders.

"No…" My voice is hoarse, breaking. "Skia would never—"

The shadows coil tighter around me, and Lucifis's eyes burn brighter.

And then the light fractures.

The world buckles, tearing me loose from the golden god's grip. Light sears everything away. I feel burning — then wake drowning in my own lungs.

I cough violently, retching up water and bile. My body convulses, each spasm wracking me until my ribs ache. The taste of metal and acid clings to my tongue, sharp and bitter. My vision swims. Every breath is a knife in my chest.

Strong hands steady me. Soft hands. Shadows wrap around me like a second skin, cool against the fever burning in my veins.

"Meir!" Skia's voice breaks through, desperate but steady, pulling me back from the chaos.

I try to stand, and I collapse against stone, the rough surface pressing into my back. My body feels broken, useless—a puppet with its strings cut. Every command I send to my limbs dissolves before it reaches them. My limbs are heavy and hard to move no matter how much my mind demands.

I cough again, gagging, my body folding in on itself. She is there immediately, kneeling, cradling me as though her touch alone can keep me from unraveling. Her face hovers over mine, her piercing green eyes blazing with a terror she refuses to voice.

"Look at me," she demands, her fingers on either side of my face, forcing my gaze to hers. "Stay with me."

Her shadows wind around me, cooling tendrils slipping across my chest, my arms, my throat. They sooth the burning fire Lucifis left inside me, cooling the fever with each pulse. They whisper calm instead of venom, an extension of her will alone.

I try to move, to sit up, to fight against the weakness crawling across my skin. My arms shake and give out beneath me, and I collapse back into her lap. Shame stings, raw and bitter.

She does not let me go. She wraps her arms tighter, shadows curling around us both, as though she can shield me from the gods themselves.

Her forehead presses to mine. Her lips find my brow, soft and lingering, carrying the weight of every unspoken vow. "Rest," she whispers, voice breaking. "Your body needs rest. Tell me everything later. But for now, please—rest for me."

Her plea carves through me, deeper than Lucifis's fire.

I try to speak, to protest, to promise her the world. But exhaustion wins. My eyes slide shut. Her shadows cover me, her coolness the last tether I cling to.

I surrender, not to Lucifis, not to the prophecy, but to her.

To Skia. To us. To the fragile promise of tomorrow.

FORTY-NINE
SKIA

I sit among the ruins with his head heavy in my lap. His skin is clammy, tacky with sweat, his tunic stiff with bile. He needs a bath, a healer, time—but all I can give him is my presence. My fingers stroke absently through his damp hair as though touch alone can knit him back together.

The late sun slants low, filtering through broken columns and dangling vines. Every crack in the stone oozes shadow, stretching long across the floor until it wraps us in its chill. Somewhere behind, Kain and Lucile whisper, their hushed tones threading unease into the silence.

I rest my head back against the ruin wall. The cool stone is a fleeting relief. My body begs for sleep, and for a breath, I surrender.

When I open my eyes again, Lucile is kneeling beside me. Her crimson gaze is rimmed dark, hollow. Dirt streaks her cheeks; her movements are mechanical, as if something else guides her bones. Shadows cling to her shoulders like a mantle.

I glance down. Meir still breathes—steady now, color inching back to his face. Carefully, I shift his head onto my cloak, a makeshift pillow. My legs prickle with pins and needles as I stand. Stones crunch under my boots as I cross to Kain. Lucile follows in silence, her presence unsettling, too vacant.

"What's wrong?" My voice is hoarse, rough by sleep and worry.

Kain's face is grave, his brow furrows deeper than I have ever seen. "Lucile had a vision. The Hunters are out. Whatever happened here ... they are searching. I think that whatever happened to Meir did something to the magic. We already know that your father is after you, and the Hunters are working for him. They will find us if we linger." His jaw tightens. "For your safety—for my queen and king's safety—we must return to the Light

Lands. Meir is not in a state to fight. Our safest place is in Luminaria."

The vines above rustle as though stirred by unseen hands. My shadows tense at my feet, pooling thicker.

I return to Meir, kneeling, patting his cheek gently. I shake him until he is dragged from sleep. "Wake, Meir."

His eyes flutter, heavy-lidded but alive. "My little shadow," he breathes

Relief surges, making me weak. "Can you move?"

He nods, though his limbs tremble. Together, we rise. His weight sagging against me, mine steady only because I refuse to falter. My shadows hold him up, taking most of the weight.

His hand in mine is clammy, yet he grips it tight as though anchoring himself.

We pause, catching our breath, as the weight of exhaustion hangs between us. Lucile hovers nearby, her gaze flickering to the edge of the ruins where our scattered packs lie half-buried among the weeds. I nod to her, and she moves with mechanical precision, gathering what's left—bedrolls, the battered satchel, Meir's sword—which she presses into my arms without a word.

Kain moves to help, his movements tense but determined. He lifts Meir's cloak, shaking off the dust, and slings it over his own shoulder. My shadows flicker, snaking out to retrieve the flask that rolled beneath a broken arch. The simple act of collecting our things feels monumental, as if each item retrieved is a promise. We will keep moving; we will not be caught here.

Once everything is gathered, I scan the treeline, searching for the horses we'd lost in the chaos. The underbrush is dense, the shadows thick and restless. Lucile moves ahead, her eyes scanning the gloom. A distant whicker and the soft crunch of hooves on dead leaves draw us forward, hearts thumping with hope and anxiety.

We forge into the forest's edge, calling softly, coaxing the frightened animals. My voice is gentle; my shadows silent and watchful. After a tense moment, the familiar shapes of our horses emerge from behind a tangle of brambles—ears flicking, eyes wide. Relief floods through me. Kain strokes one mare's neck, murmuring comfort, and Lucile steadies the other, looping the reins into Kain's palm. Meir sags against me, grateful, as I help him mount his horse.

With everything gathered and our horses finally found, we climb into the saddles. Unprepared for what the forest might hide in its shadows.

Meir's strength slowly returns, but he is exhausted. Every ounce of energy is sucked out of him, Lucile used her healing words, but they did little to help him. Though his body is weak I can feel his power. It grows and buzzes. My shadows feel it thrum. They whisper in my ear.

He will betray you, his powers are too strong.

He is unworthy.

The hiss and throb of my shadows needle the edges of my mind, insistent and relentless. I squeeze Meir's hand a little tighter, anchoring myself in the present, fighting the urge to recoil from the warnings that slither through my thoughts. He doesn't meet my eyes, his own gaze distant, lost somewhere beyond the sheltering trees. Lucile glances at us with a frown, sensing the tension but saying nothing. The forest is silent except for the soft footfalls of our horses and the rustle of leaves, a hush that feels both protective and suffocating.

I shake off the whispers, though their doubt lingers. "Meir," I murmur, my voice barely louder than the breeze, "hold on. We're almost through."

He nods, but his shoulders sag, weariness etched in every line of his body. Yet beneath it all, the pulse of his power is unmistakable—a current I can't ignore, vibrating through the air between us. My shadows recoil, wary, uncertain if his strength is a promise or a threat.

Kain rides ahead, sword resting across his lap, always alert. Lucile walks beside me, her healing words spent, her brow furrowed in concern. "We need to make camp soon," she says quietly. "He can't go much farther."

But stopping means risking discovery. My shadows flicker with agitation, stirring unease in my chest. I weigh the warnings against the trust that once bound us all together. Meir's grip tightens suddenly on my arm, his breath coming in shallow bursts. "I'm ... trying," he whispers, the words trembling.

I lean closer, letting my shadows melt away from suspicion, just for a moment. "You're not alone," I promise, willing myself to believe it. The forest presses in, ancient and secretive, and the night ahead is thick with possibility—and peril.

We ride deeper into the gloom, the past, and future trembling in the silent promise of Meir's power, and the uncertain loyalty flickering in the darkness between us.

We make it further down the path, the struggle weighing on Meir. Deciding we need to make camp so he can rest. Lucile sets up our camp. Kain helps me get Meir onto his pack. Quickly exhaustion takes over his body and he sleeps.

FIFTY
SEER

The cold, damp dungeon holds me captive with iron chains. My teeth tear at my lips, a nervous habit born of fear. Filth clings to me, the stench of sweat and blood wrapping tight around my body until even breathing feels like suffocation. Days blur into one endless nightmare. The rough stone scrapes my back, an unyielding reminder that I am trapped, and the chill of it seeps into my bones.

His fists come in silence, the rhythm of violence so familiar I can expect the next strike before it lands. Each blow chips away at me, not just flesh but spirit. Yet fists are not his sharpest weapon.

His shadows curl into my mind. They twist my visions until prophecy becomes indistinguishable from nightmare. He makes me see Skia over and over—her laughter breaking into screams, her light smothered, her soul in chains. I tell myself they are false, but each vision leaves me splintered, my hope bleeding away. My gift, once sacred, a bridge between gods and mortals, is his torment now. He tears futures from me like pages ripped from a book, demanding I surrender the threads of fate.

Every secret I give him becomes another chain tightening around my daughter's life. He knows. He knows she is my weakness. He dangles her before me as bait, weaponizing the love I have for her. When I finally break and whisper the truth—that Skia is mine, born of both illumination and shadows he smiles.

That smile is worse than any blow.

Instead of mercy, he delights in it. He sees in her what he cannot break in me.

"Is she mine?" he growls. "Did you keep her from me? Abandon me for power and not even tell me the child's power tethered to my life is born of my own blood?" he yells.

"Morthal you hold no power over me, but I hold all the power over you," I spit. "I left a weapon, a gift from the gods, my gift not yours!" I yell, my words carrying the strength my body cannot.

"That day I left her, I planted a seed that will take over from the inside and destroy all that this land stands for," I say as my eyes glare into his silver eyes.

"Oh, silly Cora," he whispers against my ear, his rancid breath turning my stomach. "You will watch her fall as each person close to her betrays her, just wait. I'll give her to Riven as his wife. Riven will take her soul piece by piece, until her shadows turn against her. Until there is nothing left but darkness."

I flinch when his grip tightens on my arm, bruising bone. No one has called me by that name since I burned it away. The air thickens with his anticipation.

"You do not get to speak my old name. You may chain me, beat me, but you will never take control of me again." The words cut, slicing every hint of our past, bleeding out into the open. "You will never hold me under your spell again, Morthal. I'm stronger than I was before you." He says nothing.

The silence after is worse than his voice. Heavy. Absolute. My heartbeat thunders, frantic against the quiet. My chains rattle when I tremble, the sound swallowed quickly by the dark.

Then the shadows shift.

He stands, my eyes watching him. With each move his shadows spread. He leans against the stone wall of the dungeon. His silver eyes glow, harsh and inhuman. His shadows creep toward me. I watch as they slither like snakes, inching closer with each breath I take. They breach my feet, the icy hands climbing my legs. Soon the shadows cover my entire body. Their hands twisting around my neck.

FIFTY-ONE
SKIA

I lie next to Meir. He sleeps soundly, not a sound disturbs him. Insomnia plagues me, an energy pulling me towards something. My shadows wake, threatening to break through the surface. I stare up at the sky, trying to ignore this pull.

My thoughts drift to Raven, my anchor in every storm. I miss her more fiercely than I can bear. She will listen, offering comfort without judgment. I long for her laughter, her steady voice, the way she can cut through my chaos. I wonder if she is looking at the same stars. Will I ever see her again?

Sleep comes jagged, uneasy. I toss, restless in the oppressive dark of the forest. The silence here is alive, whispering, watching. A tug pulls me from my sleep. My skin prickles, heart pounding with the certainty that something calls me. The pull is unbearable.

I rise, my body incapable of making any other choice and drift into the woods, compelled by a force I do not understand. Lights beckon me forward, my vision blurs as if by a dream. My legs move of their own volition. I feel as if a rope is dragging me through the forest. My legs scrape against limbs, causing blood to trickle down my skin, leaving a trail behind me. The ancient trees loom, skeletal fingers reaching down. With each step I take, the grass bends beneath my feet, the ache of stones grinding into the arches of my feet. My body does not react; it continues through the pain.

The forest thickens around me. Humming, the air grows charged with foreign energy. The silence is broken by the echo of wings. A heavy, rhythmic beat overhead. The air changes with each beat. My gaze snaps up. A monstrous hawk, wingspan blotting out the stars, swoops across the canopy. Its screech splits the silence, a sound that seems to rip at the fabric of reality itself.

Glowing orbs appear, dragging me forward like I am attached to a rope, and someone is at the other end. The forest breaks to reveal a glade. Each step toward the center leaves my feet coated in scrapes and a buzz of pain in the periphery of my mind. The lights surround the circle of the forest, entrapping me. Glowing knives flicker around the edges.

The hawk lands with a bone-shaking thud, a gust of wind ruffling the air. He shifts, yellow eyes glaring, a predatory intensity. Feathers peel away, a sickening crack as bones contort, the beak melting into a cruel, angular face. The air thickens with the coppery tang of blood and the acrid smell of smoke as he becomes a man, his skin a tapestry of black tattoos, charred along his arms and chest. A hard light surrounds him, reflecting in gleaming eyes. His teeth are stark white against his dark skin. Muscles ripple beneath black leather trousers, hands twisting into claws, sharp and black.

As he advances, the silver chains flash, catching the light. The cruel lines of his face, etched and hard, move closer, reflected in his yellow eyes. A hunter. He is here for me.

"Sweet Skia," he purrs, voice low and silken, sending a shiver through me. "You came so willingly. Following magic like a moth to a flame. I expected more from the daughter of shadows."

The forest caves in, suffocating darkness pressing close. Beyond the forest, a line of beasts' eyes burns, twin embers in the gloom. Their teeth, sharp daggers, gleam in the sickly, ethereal light that clings to me.

"Do you know what you are now?" he continues, circling me, his chains dragging through the dirt. He stops just in front of me, his teeth biting at my ear. "Not a princess. Not an heir. Not even a warrior. You are a warning. When I drag you back, chained and broken, your people will see what becomes of traitors."

He slams me into the bark of a tree, the air leaving my chest as I feel the tree crack against my back. My body lands in a heap on the ground. Pain radiates through my chest and up my back, bringing on a headache instantly. He crouches before me. Lifting my face with his rough hands, his sharp claws digging into my chin. "You should have been a good girl. You should have stayed in your home and kept the questions to yourself." He pushes me back. My body falling onto the ground. He grabs my wrists. With the manacles alive and humming, he locks them. Bringing my wrists together. Pain bursts up my arms as the chains dig into flesh.

"I am already cast out!" I hiss, my voice shaking with rage. "I am nothing to him! A pawn he discarded!"

He laughs, the sound sharp and cruel. "Cast out? Forgotten? No, sweet Skia. You were never meant to be gone. He doesn't want you lost. He wants you ruined. He wants you begging. When he finds that you've got a mate, and completed the bond ... oh Skia, you have been a very naughty girl."

He leans back, his arms crossed as he looks at me. His tongue sliding against the fang of his teeth. I look up at him, the words seething behind my teeth, "He will come for me."

He smiles and then his boot slams into the center of my chest shoving me back into the tree. Air whooshes from my lungs in a violent cough and my body falls forward from the impact on the tree. My face scrapes against the rocks on the ground. I try to spit the dirt from my mouth as I drag in breaths. Each burning in my lungs.

My shadows surge, lashing out instinctively, jagged tendrils snapping toward him. His magic wraps around them, each tendril in the grasp of his power. His yellow eyes flare. My shadows writhe, shrieking in my head, pain radiating in my body. He is attacking my shadows. They recoil, retreating close to my skin, trembling like frightened animals.

He seizes my jaw, the rough grip a vise. The world explodes in a flash of pain as my face slams into the cold, unforgiving earth. A sickening crack echos, followed by the coppery tang of blood flooding my mouth, mingling with the gritty taste of dirt. The pain sparks tears to break the dam that I try to hold firm.

He bent close, his rancid breath scorching my ear. "Do you think your little mate will save you? He bleeds light, but light fades. Shadows always remain. Will he come to the Shadowlands to retrieve you? Put his kingdom at risk for a little shadow girl?"

"I will burn to ash before you take me back," I spit, the metallic tang of blood thick on my tongue, mingling with the gritty dirt beneath my cheek. My shackled hands claw uselessly as I try to rise. He circles, a shadow falling over me, the low rasp of his breathing a chilling counterpoint to the pounding of my heart, the predator sizing up the prey.

His smile widens. "Good. Burn. That is what he wants to see. A queen of ashes."

He slams his boot down on my leg, a guttural scream escaping my throat. Bone splinters with a sharp, tearing crack. His shadows snake across the forest floor. My eyes watching them as my head lays sideways on the ground. They slither up my legs, tiny daggers slicing my flesh as they move. Tears fall to puddles on the ground. The pain is overwhelming, and each breath I take is laced with pain climbing my body. The shadows slide like a blanket covering me. They reach my neck, and they slide down my throat, choking me.

Each scream that tries to escape my throat is suffocated by his shadows. I try to draw air, but I can't. Soon the shadows have me hanging by their hands, my body dangles until he calls upon his shadows and my body is thrown. My arms wrapped in shadows behind me, slam onto the ground and my shoulders pulled tight. His shadows retreat and I drag in air trying to fill my empty lungs. My shadows writhe around me, frantic, some trying to shield me, others whispering in poisonous tones.

You are weak.

You cannot win.

He will break you.

He kicks me again. My side feels the impact of his kick. Ribs crack. Breath comes sharp, I can't fill my chest with deep breaths as tears break past my anger.

"You think you can break me?" I croak through the blood. "I was born broken. Darkness made me."

His chuckle is cold. "Then darkness will unmake you."

He hauls me up with my hair. It feels as if my hair will rip from my scalp. He yanks me to my knees. His animal eyes glare back at me. My body will not move, my shadows deep and frantic but held hostage and unable to leave.

"Let's go home, Skia," he growls viciously. "He's waiting. And I promise you. What I've done tonight is nothing compared to what he has planned."

He drags me through the dirt. My body screams, broken bones grating. My vision blurs, light dimming, until the forest bleeds into black.

The last thing I hear before the void takes me is his whisper, curling into my ear like a blade.

"You will kneel."

Darkness claims me.

FIFTY-TWO
SKIA

As I wake my heart hammers in my ears. I am midair, the forest below changing with each movement forward. The pain is almost forgettable as I look at the height and am nauseated by the swirling clouds that surround me, their gray forms obscuring the world below.

The biting breeze chills me to my core, seeping through my clothes and raising goosebumps on my arms. The massive wings beat up and down, splashing icy air across my back. *Thump, thump, thump.* Each beat a hammer blow against my fragile hope. My body shakes uncontrollably, and my eyes pour out the tears I have been holding onto, a futile release against the mounting terror and the pain searing every inch of my body. The hawk shrieks, a sound that splits the sky, and then it releases me.

His claws let loose and I am falling into the pit of the castle. The wind rushes past my ears, my screams hidden in the howling gale. I try to call upon my shadows, willing them to brace me for the impact that is looming in front of me, the castle floor rushing up to meet my inevitable demise. Falling too fast, my body flails around me, twisting and contorting as my shadows slowly cover my body. Their shape takes form, a viscous black substance that solidifies, the palms of my shadows meeting the ground with a force that rips the air from my chest. A strangled scream escapes my lips as I roll my body over, the world spinning in a dizzying haze of pain. Every part of me is screaming, a cacophony of agony threatening to consume me.

A voice, smooth and venomous, slithers through the courtyard.

"What an entrance," Riven purrs, stepping from the shadows. His smile is sharp as a blade. "The prodigal daughter, fallen from the sky. Your father will be ... delighted."

Before I can answer, rough hands seize my hair and yank me upright. Guards loom around me, their eyes empty, their faces as pale as ash. They drag me across the blackened stone, my body utterly useless as my feet scrape across the dark stones. I can hear Riven's boots clink behind me as I am dragged through the castle. The corridors of the keep pulse with veins of darkness, whispers crawling along the walls in voices that aren't human. *Pawn. Heir. Traitor.*

My body slips in and out of conscience. Each time my eyes open, I am in a different part of the castle. The throne room spreads wide, lit only by braziers of indigo fire that hiss and spit sparks of shadow. The blue umber flame makes the room feel eerie. I am thrown at the foot of the throne. Chains clink as I land. My body pitches forward, the rough stone floor scrapes against my cheek. Warm, coppery blood blooms beneath me.

"Your Highness," I am greeted by the cold, mocking voice of Riven. He stands above me, his face contorted into a cruel smirk as he surveys my battered form, a broken heap of defiance on the cold castle stone.

"What an entrance you made there, Skia. You fall from the sky like a gift, a twisted mockery of the gods' benevolence. Your father awaited such a miracle, believing it is a sign that answers his prayers. He yearned for you to come back into his hands, so that he could finally satiate his endless hunger, and suck the very life from your poor, fragile body."

His teeth sharp as he whispers the coldness into my ear. The pain in my body is so excruciating that I cannot take a deep breath, only shallow and rapid that causes my vision to swim with encroaching blackness around my already swollen eyes.

The impact, the betrayal, and the sheer terror of the situation conspires to steal the air from my lungs. I cann't catch my breath from the fall, much less the weight of the betrayal that presses down upon my heart.

My father, the man who should have been my protector, is going to kill me. The realization strikes me with the force of another blow, a wave of despair washing over me, nearly drowning me in its icy grip.

I will never see Meir again, nor feel the warmth of his comforting safety in his arms. For a moment I feel the tug of his bond, a tiny string that was braided into my heart. An aching heartbreak. Here, only pain, death's chilling promise, and a dark future remain.

Beneath me, the cold, unforgiving stone offers no comfort, just a brutal reminder. The very air is thick with the metallic tang of blood and the stench of Riven's malice, a suffocating cocktail that threatens to extinguish the last flicker of defiance within me. The castle, once a symbol of my heritage, now feels like a prison, a tomb where my life will be extinguished.

My body lies on the floor, a flood of blood from my nose making a river below my face. I cough as I try to breathe through the blood that pools in the back of my throat. Each breath, ragged, gurgled with blood. The torment wrapping around my body and snaking into my mind.

Am I going to die? Will I see my mate's blue eyes again? My father's feet fall into view. He is clothed in all black. The edge of his cloak brushing my face as he pushes me over to my back. Bending over me and grabbing my shirt and forcing me to my weak legs.

"Get up, you wretched waste of skin. I knew you were simply worthless, much like your mother." The words slap me across my face, worse than his act of violence, searing with the fire of betrayal.

My knees collapse, unable to maintain my strength. The words lost on my tongue, I stay quiet. Focusing on forcing the breath through my lungs. It burns like fire every time I inhale, each ragged gasp a testament to the pain that wrecks my body. I feel as if my lungs cannot fill all the way, my shadows swirling in my body, unable to move through the pain I'm thrumming with.

Nothing I have to say to him will leave my lips, as the air I struggle to fill my lungs with is more important. Through swollen eyelids I maintain eye contact with his silver eyes. His eyes are the darkest gray, and the shadows swirl within them, like a vortex threatening to swallow everything whole. I see no light or brightness in the dark gaze that meets mine. The light that thrums atop his head is a crown that burns there constantly. It calls to me. A faint whisper that is lost in the commotion.

His eyes simmer with my punishment, his shadows whispering loudly, promising a fate far worse than the physical torment I currently endure. His shadows leave the foot of the throne and creep toward me, tendrils of darkness slithering across the cold stone. My shadows burrow deeper inside me, knowing that his shadows will extinguish them.

The scent of blood mingles with the metallic tang of fear, a symphony of despair that echoes in the vast, silent throne room, signaling the end of what little hope I have left. I lie on my back with blood that sprays from my mouth. The healing words that Ashmore had once spoken are lost to me. Everything is fuzzy, no thoughts connect, each one falling into the darkness of the pain that screams in my brain.

His shadows wrap around my head, sinking in and devouring my thoughts. My breath quickens, and my body shakes from the torment that rips through me.

The shadows seep through my eyes, my nose, and my ears. Embrace my head, and like sharp ice, they spear through my mind, taking my thoughts. The screams from my mouth have gone hoarse as if a thousand blades rip my throat, and my brain is ice and fire.

The shadows snake through every memory. Every embrace with Meir, every betrayal I have made against my father. He sorts through each memory stealing every thought to mold into a weapon.

Then it stops. The shadows leave, my body shaking against the cold floor, the only noise that fills the throne room.

"I see you have betrayed me Skia, you bonded with the King of Light." My father's voice viciously drips with poison.

Silence, thick and heavy, descends, broken only by the frantic thudding of my heart. Then, a low chuckle, laced with amusement and something else … something dark and hungry, resonates in the air.

"My child," he laughs, the sound echoing in the sudden stillness, making me cower. I squeeze my eyes shut, desperately trying to block out the sound, but it is no use. It burrows into my very bones.

"Let the games begin. My sweet child." His voice fills the room, a dagger slicing deep.

Before I can even process the words, a blinding flash of light erupts, followed by a searing pain that explodes across my skull. I cry out, a choked gasp that is instantly lost in the overwhelming sensation. Then, darkness consumes me, a velvet blackness that swallows everything.

The pain, the fear, the echoing laughter. I feel myself falling into the abyss, the edges of my consciousness fraying and dissolving. The last thing I feel is chilling certainty. The games had indeed begun, and I was already losing.

FIFTY-THREE
MEIR

I jolt awake, heart slamming against my ribs. At first, I think it is a dream, but then I hear it. A scream. Skia's scream. It tears through the stillness of the forest, high pitched, and panic claws into my chest.

The hollow beneath the oak where we made camp is empty. My blood runs cold. I stagger to my feet, fatigue hanging on my muscles. Scanning the shadows, desperate for her, I summon my light with the energy that wakes beneath my skin. It feels stronger, charged with something more powerful weaving in and out of my light. Heavy wings came then. The sound was slow and deliberate. It tears the sky apart.

I look up through the trees.

The world falls out from under me.

There she is, Skia, caught in the talons of a massive hawk, her body limp, her shadows writhing against the crushing grip. Her body hangs limp and dread fills my chest.

My cry splits the morning air, half roar, half broken sob. I try to run toward her, but I know there is no ground that can carry me fast enough, no sword can reach that high. Kain's hands grab my shoulders, grounding me before I rip myself apart. His voice is sharp, urgent. "Meir! Listen to me—"

"What is happening?" I scream, filling the surrounding forest, and my body shakes with anger. "Where were you? How is she gone and you are here?" no evidence of a fight coats his hands.

"I don't know, Meir. We all slept through it, as if something kept us in oblivion while the very monster we were running from took her." Kain answers.

But I hear nothing. Only the rushing of blood, the fading sound of her screams, and the tearing of my heart.

"I failed her!" The words rip out of me, raw and jagged. "I failed her the way I failed my father! The shadows took him, and now they've taken her—my mate, my queen!"

Grief burns hot. Too hot.

Light explodes from me, ripping free like a star bursting apart. It sears through the clearing, forcing Kain back, driving Lucile to her knees. The earth shakes beneath me. Fireless flames erupt at my fists, scorching the forest floor until it splits in jagged cracks. The trees curl black and brittle under the assault of my fury. Within the light, daggers of shadows turn. Shadows that feel unfamiliar lace my body, almost like the sound of Skia's voice winding in them, calling for me. As if her shadows are leaving me a message of their own for me.

Kain's voice comes through the storm, faint, trembling with equal parts fear and determination. "Meir, stop! You'll burn us all! You'll burn *yourself*! If you want her back, you must master this. Control it!"

But control is gone. My vision is nothing but white fire. My body convulses as the fire burns hot and overtakes my body.

"What am I becoming?" The words rasp out of me, half prayer, half curse.

Lucile's red eyes glimmer, wide with something I have never seen from her before—fear. Kain's jaw is set tight, his knuckles white on his sword hilt, as though ready to fight me if I lose myself entirely.

I force breath into my lungs, forcing the inferno back inch by inch until I can see them again, until the forest stops screaming under my rage. My body sags, trembling, but my soul still burns.

"Lucile," I croak, "you must go back to the Shadowlands. Find out what they are doing to her. Anything. And return to me."

She hesitates. For once, the vampire has no cutting remark, only a slow nod, her expression grim.

"Is there a future that is worth saving?" I ask her. The thought breaking, "Is there a change, is this all part of some great plan the gods have failed to inform me of?" My anger boils in my blood.

Kain remains steady, his presence like a wall beside me. He puts his hand on my shoulder holding me back from my steps toward Lucile. "We will get her back, brother. You have my sword, my life. Whatever it takes."

I stare into the distance, where the sky has closed over her absence, and swear to the gods who cursed me. *I will not stop. I will not rest. I will tear the kingdoms down stone by stone until she is returned.*

The words of the golden god echo in my skull, louder than ever.

You will either break the curse or be the light that burns it all to the ground.

Maybe I am already both.

"We ride," I command, mounting before either of them can protest. "Now."

FIFTY-FOUR
MEIR

A searing rage ignites within. I will have my mate back, no matter the cost. The Shadow Lands will burn to a pile of ash and crumbling stone. Their screams will be my symphony. I'll tear their limbs and let them suffer. A fire unlike I have ever known roars in my chest—furious, relentless, consuming.

The ride back to the kingdom was a blur, days of torment and worry keeping me from restful sleep. Only stopping long enough to rest the horses. I remember only the pounding of my heart, each beat a war drum. By the time we reach the castle gates, I am off my horse, storming inside.

"Your Highness," the guards greet, bowing.

I don't slow. Their words, whispers of doubt, brush past my ears, insubstantial as the scent of wood smoke. I haven't even been crowned, but their praises, or their barbs, hold no weight. The throne, the kingdom, all mean nothing without her, the ache of her absence is a cold pressure in my chest.

My boots strike the stone floor in a feverish rhythm as I barrel into the throne room. "Send for the High Priestess, now. Summon the council. Now. Kain—bring them!" I order.

The chamber erupts into frantic motion. Pages scatter, their sandals slapping against stone as they run to do my bidding. The heat of the kingdom pounds into me, only increasing the heat against my skin. I feel like I am on fire. Kain turns on his heel, his voice sharp as he barks orders down the halls. Shadows of doubt try to creep in, but the fire blazing in my chest banishes them.

When Kain returns, the throne room beats with tension. The Priestess of Light glides forward, white robes whispering against the stone, her eyes closed as if she is already communing with the gods. Behind her, the council assembles in a tight circle, their whispers a low hum of fear and expectation.

I climb the dais and stand before the throne. The flickering candlelight dances against the vaulted walls, casting restless shadows that writhe like serpents. The scent of incense burns heavy in my lungs, mingling with the crackle of magic beginning to stir. I try to hold my magic back, knowing that the watchers still linger in my lands. It hums under my skin screaming for release.

The priestess raises her hands, sunlight catching the gold of the crown in her grasp. The intricate metalwork, crafted with symbols of the sun, shines against the stark white of the stone altar. Priestesses are the embodiment of light and innocence, their very presence a beacon of hope. Her long silver hair, streaked with highlights of gold that match the crown, sweeps down the immaculate white of her robes, the fabric almost luminous in the filtered light of the tall windows. Her eyes, the color of a summer sky, lock onto mine, their gaze both piercing and full of compassion. The silence in the vaulted hall is palpable, broken only by the distant murmur of the assembled court and the gentle crackle of torches lining the walls. Her voice, clear as a bell struck upon the purest crystal, echoes in the vast chamber. "Meir Blake Sloan of Luminaria, son of Blake Amon Sloan the King, do you accept the crown? Do you promise to protect the Light

Lands, to follow the laws of the land with mercy, and to uphold the sacred traditions of our ancestors, ensuring the Light continues to shine brightly upon this realm?"

"By the gods and the grace of my ancestors, I, Meir Blake Sloan of Luminaria, son of Blake Amon Sloan the King, accept this crown. I swear to protect the Light Lands with unwavering courage, to uphold mercy and justice in all laws, and to honor the sacred traditions passed down through generations. I pledge to safeguard the Light, so that it may forever shine upon our realm and its people," my voice, raw but steady, commands.

Her hands move with a precision that feels ancient, rehearsed by generations. She lifts the crown—crystal and gold, gleaming with inner fire—and places it upon my head. Its weight crashes down like stone, and yet it also sets my veins alight with new strength.

The priestess's voice cuts the stillness. "What will you do now, Your Majesty?"

I meet her gaze. Every shred of hesitation burns away. "I will march to war, and I will bring back my queen."

A hush settles over the throne room, every eye fixed on me, their newly crowned king. The promise hangs in the air, heavy with hope and defiance. I feel the crown's weight, not as a burden, but as a call to action. The kingdom will rise behind me, fueled by the fire I carry for her. Tonight, the Light will not waver; it will blaze forth, unyielding, until she is home once more.

FIFTY-FIVE
LUCILE

The Geheimnis Forest welcomes me back like a lover I had outgrown—its whispers familiar, its teeth just as sharp. Fog curls low across the roots, carrying with it the stench of rot and old blood. Every step I take is measured, silent, though the hunters who patrol these woods know the difference between a stray wolf and a trespasser.

I don't care. If they want to stop me, they will bleed for it.

My cloak clings to me like damp skin as I press deeper. The vision flashes behind my eyes. Her heart still beats. Faint, but there. A tremor beneath my ribs tells me she is alive. Suffering, yes—but alive. The knowledge makes my fangs ache with the promise of violence.

The castle rises from the mire like a wound in the world. Black stone slick with moss, spires twisting into the clouds, shadows leaking from its cracks like spilled ink. Hunters circle the perimeter—men, beasts, and things between. I slide into them as if I were shadow itself, a blade in the dark, silent in my kills. The taste of their blood is bitter, thick with corruption. It coats my tongue, but I swallow it down.

I slip past the gates, my body blending in with the shadows. Breathing between the iron and shadows, helps keep them from moving. The air inside is worse than the forest. Damp stone, iron, and despair. The walls themselves breathe shadows. My skin prickles. Flashes spark behind my eyes. I see the dungeon.

Down.

Always down.

My feet are silent against the stones as I make my way down each step. I need to find Skia, I need to know the state she is in.

The first thing I hear is not Skia, but the scrape of chains and a woman's broken sob. I am still pressed against the wall, peering through a crack in the torchlight. The Seer—gods, what is left of her—hangs limp, her hair matted with crimson, her golden eyes dim. Her silence screams louder than any prophecy ever has.

And then—Skia.

Her form is chained against the far wall, her body a ruin of blood and bruises. Her shadows, once alive and restless, cling faintly to her, barely flickering against the stone. My throat burns, rage, and hunger rise in tandem. But I cannot move closer. Guards linger. And worse—Riven.

He stands leaning against the dungeon wall, arms folded, his smirk a blade in the dark. His voice, smooth as poison, murmurs, "Soon," to the shadows. "Soon she will kneel. Soon she will be mine. A pretty little piece that will give me power over this kingdom."

Betrothed. The word slithers through the air unspoken, yet I feel it coil around my spine. The King of Shadows means to break her and hand her to this viper. Rage sears my veins.

I nearly launch myself into the room then, fangs bare, ready to rip him apart. But Skia lifts her head, just barely, her swollen face tilting toward the sound of his voice.

And even in that ruin, she is defiant. Her lips curl into a bloody smile. She spits at his boots.

The guard strikes her for it.

I swallow a hiss, retreating into the shadows before fury can betray me. I will not risk her life by acting now. Not yet.

I flee the way I came, slipping through corridors slick with silence, back into the choking trees of the forest. I don't breathe until the castle is a smear of black behind me. I call on my shadows and transport to Luminaria.

The city stirs, unaware that its queen-to-be bleeds in chains beneath the Shadow King's feet. I do not stop to wash, do not stop to breathe. Blood streaks my hands, shadow smoke clings to my cloak. I cover myself with shadows, I think of Kain and Meir, my shadows searching and they transport me.

Kain and Meir are already in the war room, bent over a map, their faces drawn with urgency. They both look up as I enter, their expressions shifting at once—Meir's eyes ignite, Kain's jaw tightens.

"She's alive," I rasp, my voice raw with fury. "Alive, but in the dungeons of your enemy. And worse—" I slam my bloodied hand down on the table, the map crumpling beneath it. "He means to wed her. To give her to Riven, her betrothal, he is just as dark as Morthal."

The silence after is heavy, vibrating with power, with rage, with inevitability.

Meir's light flares so bright it stings my eyes. His voice breaks like thunder. "Then we burn their kingdom to the ground."

FIFTY-SIX
MEIR

Lucile's words are knives. Skia. Shackled in the Shadow King's dungeon. Promised to Riven.

For a heartbeat, the war room freezes, the only sound is the rasp of my breath. Kain's hand tightens on the hilt of his sword, his jaw locks, but he doesn't speak. Lucile's crimson cloak is torn, her skin marked with fresh cuts, proof of how far she has gone to bring me this truth.

The bond in my chest throbs, fragile as spider-silk, but alive. She still lives. That thread is all that keeps me standing.

"Riven." His name tastes like ash and blood. My light cracks loose, spilling from my skin in ragged bursts. Torches flare so brightly the shadows retreat to the corners. I can still feel the crown heavy on my head, a reminder that I am no longer a prince. I am king—and they have stolen my queen.

Kain breaks the silence first, his voice steady but laced with steel. "Then we have no choice. It's war."

"Yes," I growl. "We gather every soldier, every banner. We ride through their shadows and burn them to ash. I will not rest until she is free."

Kain's lips curve into a grim smile. "You'll make enemies tonight, Meir."

"Good," I spit. "Let them remember why the light is something to fear."

"How are you going to gain people for a war when they do not know your queen, Meir?" Lucile asks.

"I am their king," I yell.

"I understand, but they do not have your bond. They are fearful of the Shadowlands. They were just attacked and lost one king. Do you think they will go so willingly into this battle?" she questions.

Every ounce of my body does not care. I will burn them to the ground.

"I will force them," I say.

Lucile stares and my anger becomes exhaustion because all I want is for Skia to be in my arms, safe.

"What is your plan?" I ask and she smiles.

FIFTY-SEVEN
SKIA

*M*onths ago,

The Shadowlands are always active, but the night is ours. Raven and I run barefoot through the orchard below the castle walls. Damp earth clings to our feet. We hitch our skirts in our fists and dodge the twisted trunks. The fruit hangs heavy and untouched. It glows under the moons. Each step we make feels like a step towards freedom. Our laughter is the only sound that fills the orchard. The air smells of damp soil from the night rain. It also smells of something wild. We almost believe this freedom is ours.

We collapse in the tall grass, gasping, laughter bubbling out until our ribs ache. The moons watch overhead, their mingled light painting Raven's pale skin in shifting shades. She sprawls beside me, hair tangled, her sharp grin softer in the night.

"Someday we'll leave all this behind," she whispers, her voice rough and breathless. "The castle. The rules. Even your father. We'll vanish into the forest, Skia, and it'll be ours. Not his."

I turn, prop on my elbow, studying her profile. "You sound like a queen."

Her grin widens, though her orange eyes glint like embers. "I don't need to be queen. I just need you."

The words pierce something deep inside me. Raven rarely bares herself this way. Usually, her affection is hidden behind claws and teasing smirks. But now her hand finds mine, fingers warm and calloused, gripping with a strength that almost hurts.

"Always," I whisper, the promise falling from me without hesitation. "We'll grow old together. You'll shift into a cat and terrorize the children, and I'll pretend not to see."

Her laughter rings through the orchard—bright, fierce, defiant. "Always," she echoes, like a vow.

We lay side by side, spinning dreams as though the night will never end. She swears she will never marry, never bow to anyone, that no man or woman alive could tame her. I swear I will one day cross into the Light Lands, to see if their sun really shines brighter than our moons. We share secrets that would have damned us if my father had heard, trading oaths sealed in whispers and shadows.

At some point, Raven shifts, her form folding into a sleek black cat. She curls against me, purring against my ribs, her warmth grounds me. I bury my fingers in her fur, feeling safe in a way I never feel within the castle walls. My shadows, restless and hungry, quieted with her nearby.

The castle bells toll curfew, their hollow clang stretching across the valley. Raven shifts back, her hair wild from the change, her grin wicked. She offers me her hand. When I take it, she squeezes again harder this time, her eyes sharp, daring the world to break us.

"Always," she says again.

And I believe her. With everything I have.

FIFTY-EIGHT
SKIA

I blink against the darkness, my body limp against the cold, wet stone. My head throbs, each pulse a drumbeat of pain. The air is thick, rancid, pressing into my lungs like rot given form. A single drop of water falls somewhere in the distance, echoing endlessly, mocking me with the reminder of time passing. I cannot tell how long I've been here. Hours. Days. Eternity.

My wrists burn, bound by iron so heavy it feels as though the chains themselves are alive, feeding on me. I call on my shadows but there is not even a whisper to answer. The shackles breathing them in, taking them from me. Every shift of movement sends agony screaming through my arms, my left arm useless, hanging at an unnatural angle. My face feels swollen beyond recognition, each blink sticky with dried blood that seals my lashes together.

With each breath, there is a battle. My chest rises shallow. My shadows, once my only constant, do not answer me. The silence inside my mind is worse than the chains. They've abandoned me.

The smell is musty, sour and harsh, like decay, a scent that clings to the back of my throat, making me feel ill. Every part of my body aches as I try to force my eyes open through the slits that they are. My eyelids feel swollen and heavy, glued shut by dried blood.

My body hangs, and pain overwhelms me as every part of me screams. Through the slits of my eyes, I glimpse my body slumped past my shoulder in a manner that is impossible, grotesquely abnormal. My right arm reaches over, a clumsy, desperate movement, and just the slight brush of my fingers against my torso sends a screaming pain through my body, a white-hot agony that steals my breath. I try to contort my body into something less painful. Every part of my body is in torment. I don't feel the clothes on my body, or what clothes I might have been wearing previously, and I feel exposed, vulnerable to whatever horrors the darkness might hold. I feel a knot tight in my throat, holding back the tears that threaten to spill over and betray my weakness.

Pain screams from every inch of my swollen face. I feel the lumps and the ridges of my face as I use my right hand to feel the damage, my fingers tracing the contours of a battlefield that I can't remember fighting on. I feel the slits that are still dripping with blood, the warm, sticky liquid running down my cheek, the distinction lost in the swirling vortex of pain and confusion.

The nausea that overwhelms me tumbles through my body, a violent wave that threatens to consume me, and I bend over, heaving onto the cold, unforgiving floor. My entire body is rejecting everything that I have gone through, betraying me with its weakness, and the fear that rolls in my stomach brings on more heaves of nothing but the empty air.

Through my ragged heaves, I hear the scatter of paws on the stones that surround me. The sound is so familiar, a comforting rhythm that cuts through the darkness, and I know it must be Raven. My swollen eyes prevent me from seeing if that is her, but the sound alone is enough to fill me with a surge of hope.

She found me.

My best friend is here to save me. I summon all my remaining energy, every shred of willpower, and raise myself up, trying to search the room for her, to find the source of the promising sound.

As she gets closer, my heart thunders louder in my chest, a frantic drumbeat against the silence, and my hope returns, a fragile butterfly taking flight. I think I can feel my shadows stir inside me, a faint whisper in the darkness, a flicker of recognition.

"You came for me," a whisper escapes my lips as they make it past my raw, abused throat. I can hardly utter a word, but the words are enough.

She is here.

And perhaps, just perhaps, I might survive this.

But when she speaks, the world tilts.

"I am not here to save you, Skia." Her voice is warm silk but threaded with poison. She leans close, breaths hot and rancid against my ear.

What?

No.

My stomach hits the ground as I fight the urge to vomit the bile from the back of my throat.

Betrayal sinks into my skin, prickling, leaving deep gouges against my soul. My mind feels as if claws are ripping every moment I trusted her, slamming them into my heart breaking it open.

"I am here to kill you."

For a heartbeat, I cannot breathe. My mind claws for reason. My best friend, my anchor, my sister in everything but blood. It has to be a lie. This can't—

Her breath smells rotten, and her body grew into something I had only ever seen once before. In this very dungeon. My stomach drops as my body makes the connections my mind wants to forget. I see her body morph and change, her body growing, the smell growing stronger, turning my stomach all over again. Her eyes flare bright orange, unnatural, cruel. Her body shifts, stretching, twisting, the air thickening with the scent of decay. Claws drag down my cheek in a single, deliberate stroke.

No.

No.

No, no, no.

Flesh splits. Blood spills warm and fast, dripping into my mouth, copper thick against my tongue. She lifts her hand, licks my blood with a smile too wide, too pleased. She is a monster, her bones long, and the kindness leaving her features. Her eyes meet mine, and I feel the beast she has become shake with laughter, as if this has all been a game to her. She raises her claw and slaps me across my face. I struggle to blink awake, fighting the heavy feeling in my eyes. Far off, I hear a pair of boots clank across the floor.

"Why?" The word breaks from me, ragged, desperate, my throat tearing around it.

A flash of every moment, breadcrumbs leading to this exact moment, every excuse, every promise smacks me hard against my face.

Raven's laughter shakes me harder than the blow. She contorts close, her voice low, a growl of the beast, taunting, curling into my marrow.

"Do you remember, Ski? The orchard. The moons. You asked me once if I would always stand by you." Her claws tilt my chin, forcing me to meet her glowing gaze.

"I said *always*. And I mean it." Her smile twists the shard of teeth that coats her face unnerving.

Her voice shifts, a low growl that vibrates through my bones, raising gooseflesh on my arms as the beast's shadow falls.

"Always to be your ruin. Always to watch you fall."

The memory crashes through me—grass brushing our ankles, her hand clutching mine, the words whispered like a vow. Now it shatters, jagged edges cutting deeper than her claws ever could.

My breath comes in shallow gasps, panic clawing its way up my chest. My shadows recoil, curling tighter into themselves, useless.

Boots stomp against the floor.

Slow. Heavy. Echoing against the dungeon walls, each step is irrevocable as a tolling bell.

"Oh, what a mess you are, my beautiful wife," Riven's voice snakes across the chamber, smooth and venomous. My body stiffens, dread choking what little air I have left. His shadow stretches across the floor, long and grotesque.

"No." The word is barely a sound, a plea lost in the dark.

He steps into the light, fangs gleaming, his smile cruel with satisfaction. Raven moves aside, her monstrous grin echoing his. Together, they watch me sink, watch me break, watch me fall into the abyss they had planned for me all along.

The last thing I see before the blackness takes me is his face—Riven, triumphant. And Raven's whisper, like a knife across my soul.

"Always."

To my dear readers,

When I began this journey, I didn't know if I would ever finish it. Life had other plans—ones that tested me in ways I never expected. Years ago, I faced a stroke that shook my world and left me wondering if I would ever find my way back to myself. Recovery was not just physical—it was emotional, mental, and spiritual. Every word I wrote was a fight against doubt, against fear, against the shadows that tried to silence me.

But in those shadows, I found Skia. She became my companion through the hardest moments, a reflection of resilience and survival. Her strength was born from my weakness, her fight from my struggles. Every obstacle I overcame became the ink that shaped her story. Writing her into existence wasn't just about creating a character—it was about reclaiming my voice.

This book is more than a story; it's proof that light can be born from darkness, that even when life tries to break you, you can rise, rebuild, and write your own ending. If you hold these pages in your hands, know that you, too, have the strength to face your shadows and step into the light.

Thank you for walking this path with me. Thank you for believing in stories, in survival, and in the power of never giving up.

I want to thank each ARC reader who helped me along this journey. My friends who give me a shouldder to lean on when thing get though, and my family. Without my family this would never be possible, thank you for supporting me in this next chapter.

With all my heart,

E.L. Pace

Made in the USA
Coppell, TX
27 February 2026

72466690R00215